EDUCATION
PROFESSIONALS

PRACTICAL CAREER GUIDES

Series Editor: Kezia Endsley

Dental Assistants and Hygienists, by Kezia Endsley
Education Professionals, by Kezia Endsley
Health and Fitness Professionals, by Kezia Endsley
Medical Office Professionals, by Marcia Santore

EDUCATION PROFESSIONALS

A Practical Career Guide

KEZIA ENDSLEY

ROWMAN & LITTLEFIELD
Lanham • Boulder • New York • London

Published by Rowman & Littlefield
An imprint of The Rowman & Littlefield Publishing Group, Inc.
4501 Forbes Boulevard, Suite 200, Lanham, Maryland 20706
www.rowman.com

6 Tinworth Street, London, SE11 5AL, United Kingdom

British Library Cataloguing in Publication Information Available

Library of Congress Cataloging-in-Publication Data

Names: Endsley, Kezia, 1968– author.
Title: Education professionals : a practical career guide / Kezia Endsley.
Description: Lanham : Rowman & Littlefield, [2019] | Series: Practical career guides |
   Includes bibliographical references.
Identifiers: LCCN 2018050789 (print) | LCCN 2018055665 (ebook) |
   ISBN 9781538111765 (electronic) | ISBN 9781538111758 (pbk. : alk. paper)
Subjects: LCSH: Teaching—Vocational guidance—United States. | Teachers—United States.
Classification: LCC LB1775.2 (ebook) | LCC LB1775.2 .E525 2019 (print) |
   DDC 370.71/1—dc23
LC record available at https://lccn.loc.gov/2018050789

To Christopher,
who makes me so proud

Contents

How can a young person who wants to be a teacher prepare for the experience?

You must be patient when working with others and can explain things to others—that's a really good start. You *must* have a passion for it; it's not for everyone. The burnout rate for teachers is two to three years. It's not about money. Never take the job if you're only doing it because you want summers off. Don't do it for any of those reasons, or you will be miserable.

Has the job been what you expected?

Yes. I was ready. I knew I wanted to do it. It's stable. Not too glamorous. It's very rewarding.

What would be your advice to a young person who is considering becoming a teacher?

Try to do any observing you can. Reach out to teachers who made an impact on your life; see if you can observe or shadow. Even a principal or administrator that you got along with, to make a connection so you can see what it's really like and what the teacher goes through. You can see things without the rose-colored glasses.

Also, you can take your teaching degree anywhere in the world. With certain certifications, you can teach anywhere. There are teacher shortages all over.

═══════════

Would I Be a Good Teacher?

Ask yourself these questions:

- Do I enjoy being around kids or young adults?
- Am I organized, reliable, kind, and flexible?
- Am I ready to spend most of my working day on my feet?
- Can I develop and act on teaching plans?
- Do I want to build strong relationships with students and engage with them directly?
- Do I see teaching as fun and can I bring that fun into the classroom?
- Am I a lifelong learner and excited at the prospect of continuously learning?
- Do I have a passion for the subject I will be teaching?
- Can I be a disciplinarian *and* a mentor to students?

"Remember that the content will change throughout the years but that's not a big issue. You'll always have to adapt and plan and present information in different ways. That's the easy part. Dealing with kids who are hurt or have family issues—or you get a report about a parent who's sick—helping those kids and supporting them is the challenging (and most important) part."—Karen Canning, seventh grade teacher

If the answer to any of these questions is an adamant *no*, you might want to consider a different path. Remember that learning what you *don't* like can be just as important as figuring out what you *do* like to do.

Teachers can be mentors, friends, and inspirations to their students.

CHARACTERISTICS OF SUCCESS IN THE EDUCATION FIELD

Regardless of the type of teaching you choose, there are commonalities that all people who enjoy success as a teacher share. Consider how well the following phrases describe who you are:

- Enjoy helping people, especially children
- Are organized and self-motivated
- Are flexible
- Get fulfillment from helping others
- Not financially motivated
- Enjoy cooperative and collaborative work
- Feel comfortable being in charge
- Feel comfortable motivating others
- Empathetic toward struggle and kind to others
- Get energy from being around others
- Enjoy learning

Remember that if you pursue a career that fundamentally conflicts with the person you are, you won't be good at it and you won't be happy. Don't make that mistake. If you need help in determining your key personality factors, you can take a career counseling questionnaire to find out more. You can find many online or ask your school guidance counselor for reputable sources.

Summary

In this chapter, you learned a lot about the different types of teaching positions that exist in the United States. You've learned about what teachers do in elementary, middle, and high school, as well as some pros and cons about teaching, the average salaries of these jobs, and the outlook in the future for teaching. You hopefully even contemplated some questions about whether your personal likes and preferences meld well with being a teacher. At this time, you should have a good idea about which age group you might prefer to teach, and maybe you even know the subject matter you want to teach. Are you starting to get excited about the idea of being a teacher? If not, that's okay, as there's still time.

An important takeaway from this chapter is that no matter which kind of teaching you choose, you need to have a passion for teaching in order to succeed. Being a teacher isn't just a job, it's a calling. It's who you are. You will save yourself and your potential students some grief if you recognize before you start that teaching doesn't fit your aspirations. In addition, you need to have a lifelong love of learning to succeed in the education profession.

Chapter 2 dives into forming a plan for your future, covering everything there is to know about educational requirements, certifications, internship and student teaching requirements, and more, about each of these areas of teaching. You'll learn about finding summer jobs and making the most of volunteer work as well. The goal is for you to set yourself apart—and above—the rest.

2

Forming a Career Plan

*N*ow that you have some idea what teaching is all about—and maybe you even know which type of teaching you are interested in—it's time to formulate a career plan. For you organized folks out there, this can be a helpful and energizing process. If you're not a naturally organized person, or if the idea of looking ahead and building a plan to adulthood scares you, you are not alone. That's what this chapter is for.

After discussing ways to develop a career plan—there is more than one way to do this!—the chapter dives into the various educational requirements. Finally, it looks at how you can gain experience through classroom shadowing, student teaching, volunteering, camp counseling, babysitting, and more. Yes, experience will look good on your résumé, and in some cases it's even required, but even more important, getting out there and working with children or young adults in various settings is the best way to determine whether teaching is really something that you will enjoy. When you find a career that you truly enjoy and have a passion for, it will rarely feel like work at all.

If you still aren't sure if teaching is right for you, try a self-assessment questionnaire or a career aptitude test. There are many good ones on the web. As an example, the career resource website Monster.com includes free self-assessment tools at www.monster.com/career-advice/article/best-free-career-assessment-tools. The Princeton Review also has a very good aptitude test geared toward high schoolers at www.princetonreview.com/quiz/career-quiz.

Your ultimate goal should be to match your personal interests and goals with your preparation plan for college and career. Practice articulating your plans and goals to others. When you feel comfortable doing this, that means you have a good grasp of your goals and your plan to reach them.

Planning the Plan

You are on a fact-finding mission of sorts. A career fact-finding plan, no matter what the field, should include these main steps:

- Take some time to consider and jot down your interests and personality traits. Are you a people person, or do you get energy from being alone? Are you creative or analytical? Are you outgoing or shy? Are you organized or creative—or a little of both? Take a career counseling questionnaire (found online or in your guidance counselor's office) to find out more. Consider whether your personal likes and preferences meld well with the jobs you are considering.
- Find out as much as you can about the day-to-day work of teachers at all levels. In what kinds of environments do they work? Who do they work with? How demanding is the job? What are the challenges? Chapter 1 of this book is designed to help you in this regard.
- Find out about educational requirements and schooling expectations. Will you be able to meet any rigorous requirements? This chapter will help you understand the educational paths and licensing requirements of teaching.
- Seek out opportunities to volunteer or shadow teachers doing the job. Use your critical thinking skills to ask questions and consider whether this is the right environment for you. This chapter also discusses ways to find job-shadowing opportunities, summer jobs working with kids, and other job-related experiences.
- Look into student aid, grants, scholarships, and other ways you can get help to pay for schooling. It's not just about student aid and scholarships, either. There are programs available designed specifically to help potential teachers get their degrees; for example, if you are willing to teach underserved populations such as in predominately black or Native American districts, you may be eligible to receive educational grants and funding for school. Check out the US Department of Education website at https://studentaid.ed.gov/sa/types/grants-scholarships/teach for more information or search online for information about the Teacher Education Assistance for College and Higher Education (TEACH) Grant.

- Build a timetable for taking required exams such as the SAT and ACT, applying to schools, visiting schools, and making your decision. You should write down all important deadlines and have them at the ready when you need them.
- Continue to look for employment that matters during your college years—internships and work experiences that help you get hands-on experience and knowledge about your intended career.
- Find a mentor who is currently teaching the subject or grade level you are interested in. This person can be a great source of information, education, and connections. Don't expect a job (at least not at first); just build a relationship with someone who wants to pass along his or her wisdom and experience. Coffee meetings or even e-mails are a great way to start.

"Find something you really are passionate about to teach. There is something about teaching a subject matter that you love to someone else so they can engage with it that is amazing."—Jeff Hegnauer, fourth grade teacher

A mentor can help you in many ways.

Where to Go for Help

If you're aren't sure where to start, your local library, school library, and guidance counselor's office are great places to begin. Search your local or school library for resources about finding a career path and finding the right schooling that fits your needs and budget. Make an appointment with or e-mail a counselor to ask about taking career interest questionnaires. With a little prodding, you'll be directed to lots of good information online and elsewhere. You can start your research with these four sites:

- The Bureau of Labor Statistics Career Outlook site at www.bls.gov/career outlook/home.htm. The US Department of Labor's Bureau of Labor Statistics site doesn't just track job statistics, as you learned in chapter 1. An entire section of the BLS website is dedicated to helping young adults looking to uncover their interests and to match those interests with jobs currently in the market. Check out the section called "Career Planning for High Schoolers." Information is updated based on career trends and jobs in demand, so you'll get practical information as well.
- The Mapping Your Future site at www.mappingyourfuture.org. This site helps you determine a career path and then helps you map out a plan to reach those goals. It includes tips on preparing for college, paying for college, job hunting, résumé writing, and more.
- The Education Planner site at www.educationplanner.org. With separate sections for students, parents, and counselors, this site breaks down the task of planning your career goals into simple, easy-to-understand steps. You can find personality assessments, get tips on preparing for school, read Q&As from counselors, download and use a planner worksheet, read about how to finance your education, and more.
- The TeenLife site at www.teenlife.com. Calling itself "the leading source for college preparation," this site includes lots of information about summer programs, gap year programs, community service, and more. Promoting the belief that spending time out "in the world" outside of the classroom can help students do better in school, find a better fit in terms of career, and even interview better with colleges, this site contains lots of links to volunteer and summer programs.

Use these sites as jumping-off points and don't be afraid to reach out to a real person, such as a guidance counselor or your favorite teacher, if you're feeling overwhelmed.

TEACHING IS IN HER BLOOD

Shanna Mattax

Shanna Mattax graduated from Indiana University–Purdue University at Indianapolis (IUPUI) in 2008 with an elementary education degree and a concentration in reading. She started working as Title I instructional assistant (K–1 reading intervention). She has been teaching first grade in the same school district in a mid- to large-size rural area for the past ten years.

Can you explain how you became interested in being a teacher?

On my dad's side of the family, there are lots of educators and people who have been involved in education. I can't remember a time when I wasn't interested in being a teacher. I played "teacher" a lot when I was a kid. I had a lot of amazing teachers growing up, too, which solidified my interest in teaching. Once I got into the block system after my first year of college and started student teaching, I knew it was really what I wanted to do. I loved how the teachers made a difference in kids' lives. I wanted to do that and I knew I would be good at it!

What is a typical day in your job?

I start with morning work with my kids to get our day off on the right foot. Then we do intervention groups so kids can work on specific skills that they haven't yet mastered. After that, we have a ninety-minute reading block, where the kids work through literacy stations. Then it's lunch and recess time. In the afternoon, we focus on writing, science, and social studies. Finally, they have specials (music, art, STEM [science, technology, engineering, and mathematics], and gym). We finish off with math stations and an end-of-the-day meeting and then the kids go home. Then I usually stay about an hour longer (as well as about an hour and a half in the morning before school). During that prep time, I have meetings with teachers, leadership meetings, or I am working on next week's plans, or getting ready for that day. After school, I'm finishing up the day and doing plans for the upcoming weeks.

Can you talk more about the great teachers in your past who really moved you?

My third grade and fifth grade teachers were especially great! They knew all of the kids. They took time out of their lunchtime to eat with us sometimes when we met certain goals. They cared about the kids. You could tell that they loved teaching, and it showed. They were fun; they were energetic. It was a fun place to be every day, but you were also at school. I have some great memories during those times.

How is elementary education different, and why did you pick it?

I always wanted to do elementary education because I connect really well with younger kids. I choose primary (K–2) because I like teaching kids to read. My awesome teachers in my past fostered my love of reading. I got my reading concentration on top of my degree, because I wanted my focus to be teaching kids to read. Elementary education is great in general because it's very hands-on. The kids really love school at this point and they love their teachers at this age. They just soak up everything that you tell them. They are so impressionable so I wanted to be a great model. You always remember your elementary school teachers.

What is the best part of your job?

The biggest thing is being able to share my love of learning with young kids. For most of them, this is their second year in school learning. Being able to share how much I love it and share the days with them is amazing. Seeing them learn and grow throughout the year is so wonderful. As they age and move from grade to grade, they will still wave to me in the hallways. Seeing the growth they make throughout the years is really rewarding.

What is the most challenging part of your job?

Making sure that I am meeting all their needs—academic, social, and emotional. Making sure I am reaching all of my kids and doing the best for each one while they are in my classroom. To address these challenges, I try to build a strong relationship with the student and their family from the start, so then the parents will be comfortable talking to me if they need support.

Also, working with people in the building when one of my kids needs additional support that I can't give them is key. I can reach out to others so we can help the student as a team. Working with other teachers to bounce off ideas and support each other in helping the kids is really helpful. I constantly check with my kids and see how they are doing so I can determine their emotional state and address any problems or issues.

Did your education prepare you for the job?

It gave me a good foundation and a glimpse as to if I would have the passion for this job. Some days are hard, and it does take a lot of extra hours out of the classroom. It showed me what I would teach and if I could deal with it. Student teaching and observing hands-on were really the most valuable. I did observing one day a week on and off for two years. I did true student teaching one semester for two years (so twice). The last one was focused on reading. Working directly with the kids was the most valuable for me.

Why did you pursue the reading endorsement?

My love of reading drew me to it. It's not as common to get an endorsement, but I knew that I wanted to teach primary and that it does help in gaining employment. I had to take more classes, and it sets you apart. I had to have special permission to take more classes on top of my block. It shows employers that I had more education in reading. If you can get extra classes, an endorsement, or a dual license, you will have an edge.

Has the job been what you expected it to be?

It changes so much. It is what I expected when it comes to working with the kids and the passion that I knew I would have. It's now less about teachers teaching the class and more student-led, where the kids do the stations based on their needs. Now we differentiate kids' abilities more and they work on what they need to work on. They are more in charge of their learning, which they really like.

What would be your advice to a young person who is considering becoming a teacher?

Make sure you have the passion for it. Some days are going to be trying, but it's worth it. Don't ever stop learning—always look for more things you can do to help your kids. It's all about collaboration. Find a way to spend some time in the classroom while you are in high school and get some real-life experience. See if you like the whole feeling of the school and being with the kids. Don't wait until you get to the end of college and you are student teaching. Go and observe and see if you like it—try cadet teaching! Last of all, do it! We need more great, passionate teachers!

Making High School Count

Regardless of the career you choose, if you are interested in teaching, there are some basic yet important things you can do while in high school to position yourself in the most advantageous way. Remember—it's not just about having the best application, it's also about figuring out which areas of teaching you actually would enjoy and which ones don't suit you.

- Sign up for cadet teaching experiences if your high school offers such classes. If not, take the initiative to seek out time in the classroom of a teacher you really liked in the past.
- Start tutoring age-appropriate students in the subject matter you're passionate about.
- Use the summers to get as much experience working with kids as you can. Babysitting, summer camps, parks and recreation departments, and local YMCAs are all good places to work with kids and learn how they tick.
- Learn first aid and CPR. You'll need these important skills regardless of your profession.
- Hone your communication skills in English, speech, and debate. You'll need them to speak with everyone from students to administrators.
- Volunteer in as many settings as you can. Read on to learn more about this important aspect of career planning.

Educational Requirements

The nice thing is that, with some exceptions, you can enter the teaching profession with many different bachelor's degrees. (More information about transition-to-teaching programs is included later in this chapter.) As long as you are certified in the state in which you want to teach, you don't always need a traditional education bachelor's degree. The following sections cover the traditional educational requirements in detail, and then cover a few exceptions as well.

EDUCATIONAL REQUIREMENTS FOR ELEMENTARY EDUCATION TEACHERS

Elementary education teachers are qualified to teach students in kindergarten through sixth grade, instructing students in a wide range of subjects, including reading, math, science, social studies, and writing.[1] If you want to teach in a publicly funded school, you will be required to hold a bachelor's degree, traditionally in elementary education. Some states also require elementary education teachers to have majored in a specific content area, such as English or math.

You also need a certificate or license issued by the state in which you want to teach. Most states require you pass the PRAXIS certification exams, but some states, such as Indiana and Illinois, have their own tests and requirements. For more information about the certification process, see the sidebar "The Teacher Certification Process."

Private school teachers may not be required to meet these same standards, and the requirements can vary depending on the school. Teachers in these schools are typically required to hold a bachelor's degree, but may not be required to be certified or licensed.

The student-teaching experience, which typically takes place during the last semester of your degree program, is an important part of your education. As a student teacher you will be placed into a real classroom of students, where you will teach under the supervision of an experienced teacher who guides you—at least initially. You may end up taking over and teaching the class entirely, with only intermittent supervision and mentoring from your teacher. This is an important experience that will help you start to develop your teaching style and your goals as a teacher. This is where you'll start to develop the soft skills—such as flexibility—that are important to have in the classroom. See the section "Making the Most of Your Student Teaching Experience" for lots more about student teaching.

During your educational process, you will work as a student teacher in a classroom.

THE TEACHER CERTIFICATION PROCESS

In addition to the degree requirements to become a teacher, all states have certification requirements for teaching in public schools, which often vary depending on the age group or subject area you want to teach. (If you plan to teach only in private schools, you may not need a license.) You may need to take a state-approved teacher preparation program and then sign up for and pass the required exams. You will need to pass the general teaching certification test, and you will probably also be required to pass a test that proves your knowledge of the subject you will teach.

To find out what you need to do in your state of residence, start with these sites:

- ETS PRAXIS Tests State Requirements (www.ets.org/praxis/states), which includes a clickable list of US states and territories, where you can find specific information about certifications and licensing requirements
- Certification Map: Teacher Certification Made Simple! at (https://certification map.com/states), a more comprehensive site lists and explains the licensing requirements in each state
- Teach.org (www.teach.org), which includes lots of information about becoming a teacher, including certification and licensing requirements, career paths, salary and benefits, funding your education, and more

Once you become licensed, you will be eligible to work as a substitute teacher. Some states allow you to teach without a license as long as you have a certain number of college credit hours. This is a great way to get experience in a variety of settings and beef up your résumé as you are looking for a full-time position. Substitute teaching can provide indispensable experience working with different grade levels, subjects, and student populations.

EDUCATIONAL REQUIREMENTS FOR MIDDLE SCHOOL TEACHERS

Pursuing the secondary education track (as opposed to elementary/primary education) will qualify you to teach middle school and high school students. You then determine which age group you prefer to teach during your student-teaching experiences and by the specific courses you take when pursuing your education degree.

Middle school teachers typically teach students in sixth through eighth grade. They typically instruct students in one specialized area, such as math or Spanish, for example. The most common way to prepare to teach middle school is to get an undergraduate degree in your subject of choice (such as math) with a minor/concentration in education.[2]

This usually means that you will declare an interest in teaching by applying to the education program early in your college career. This process often includes an essay and interviews to determine your suitability and desire to teach. A minor in education typically translates to twenty-seven credit hours of education coursework, some of which is specific to the grade level you plan to teach. The student-teaching experience, which typically takes place during the last semester of your degree program, is an important part of your education. It is discussed in more detail in the section "Making the Most of Your Student Teaching Experience."

If you want to teach in a publicly funded school, you will be required to hold a bachelor's degree regardless of the grade level you teach. Some states and individual schools also require that you earn a master's degree in a related area within a certain amount of time after you become employed as a secondary education teacher.

You also need a certificate or license issued by the state in which you want to teach. Most states require you pass the PRAXIS certification exams, but some states have their own tests and requirements. For more information about the certification process, see the sidebar "The Teacher Certification Process."

As mentioned earlier, private school teachers may not be required to meet the same standards, and the requirements can vary depending on the school.

EDUCATIONAL REQUIREMENTS FOR HIGH SCHOOL TEACHERS

To teach at the high school level (grades 9–12), you must pursue the secondary education track (as opposed to elementary/primary education), as discussed in the previous section. This process will qualify you to teach both middle school and high school students. You then determine which age group you prefer to teach during your student-teaching experiences and by the specific courses you take when pursuing your education degree.

"The education process prepares you for the 'content' portion of teaching, but nothing really prepares you to teach better than on-the-job experience."—Denise Cotton, high school chemistry teacher

High school teachers typically instruct students in one specialized area, such as math or biology, for example. You will be required to hold an undergraduate degree in your subject of choice, with a minor or concentration in education.[3]

This usually means that you will declare an interest in teaching by applying to the education program early in your college career. This process often includes an essay and interviews to determine your suitability and desire to teach. A minor in education typically translates to about twenty-seven credit hours of education coursework, some of which is specific to the grade level you plan to teach. The student-teaching experience, which typically takes place during the last semester of your degree program, is an important part of your education. It is discussed in more detail in the section "Making the Most of Your Student Teaching Experience."

If you want to teach in a publicly funded school, you will be required to hold a bachelor's degree to be a teacher, regardless of the grade level you teach. Some states and school corporations also require that you earn a master's degree in a related area within a certain amount of time after you become employed as a secondary education teacher.

If you already have a bachelor's degree and want to leave your current profession to become a teacher, many transition-to-teaching programs exist that can help you achieve the requirements and credentials to teach in one year. For example, the state of Indiana offers a two-semester transition-to-teaching program that prepares career professionals with bachelor's degrees to teach middle or high school classes.[4]

You also need a certificate or license issued by the state in which you want to teach. Most states require you pass the PRAXIS certification exams, but some states have their own tests and requirements. For more information about the certification process, see the sidebar "The Teacher Certification Process."

As mentioned earlier, private school teachers may not be required to meet the same standards, and the requirements can vary depending on the school.

"Don't just be the leader, but also let the students guide and find their own way."
—Greg Wilson, seventh grade teacher

BEING A TEACHING ASSISTANT

Becoming a teaching assistant (also called a *teacher's aide*, *instructional aide*, *para-professional*, *education assistant*, or *paraeducator*) is a good way to step slowly into teaching. Teaching assistants, who typically need to have completed about two years of college-level coursework to work in a classroom, work under the guidance of the main teacher to provide students with additional instruction.

Common tasks that teaching assistants do include:

- Reinforcing lessons presented by teachers by reviewing material with students one-on-one or in small groups
- Setting up teaching equipment and preparing materials for the teacher
- Supervising students in class, between classes, during lunch and recess, and on field trips
- Helping teachers with record keeping, such as tracking attendance and calculating grades[5]

Some teaching assistants work only with special education students. In some cases, these special education students attend regular classes, and teaching assistants help them understand the material and adapt the information to their learning style. If you are interested in becoming a special education teacher, this paid position is a great way to gain experience in the field before you commit to the full educational requirements to become a teacher.

Teacher's assistants sometimes work with students with special needs.

EDUCATIONAL REQUIREMENTS FOR OTHER SPECIALIST TEACHERS

If you are interested in a special area of teaching, you may be required to have additional education or credentials. For example, consider the requirements of these specialized areas of teaching, which were introduced and explained in chapter 1:

- *Special education teachers:* In addition to the basic requirements to teach at the appropriate grade level, discussed previously, many states require that you earn a degree specifically in special education. You'll learn about the different types of disabilities and how to teach information so that your students will understand. To become fully certified, some states also require special education teachers to complete a master's degree in special education after obtaining a job.
- *ESL teachers:* In addition to the basic requirements to teach at the appropriate grade level, discussed previously, most states require that ESL teachers have some type of certification or license. Likewise, public schools often require their ESL teachers to hold an ESL endorsement.
- *Physical education teachers:* In addition to the basic requirements to teach at the appropriate grade level, discussed previously, many states require that physical education teachers have a concentration or minor in physical education.
- *Art teachers:* The most traditional way to become an art teacher is to pursue a bachelor's degree in art education. As with general studies, you will need to determine whether you would like to teach art at the elementary or secondary level. To obtain a secondary education degree, you will likely be required to major in art and minor in art education.
- *Music teachers:* The most traditional way to become a music teacher is to pursue a bachelor's degree in music education. As with general studies, you will need to determine whether you would like to teach art at the elementary or secondary level. To obtain a secondary education degree, you will likely be required to major in music and minor in music education.
- *Foreign language teachers:* To teach a foreign language, you must have a bachelor's degree in the language (unless you are otherwise fluent) and a teaching certification. Most schools districts will also insist that you have experience living and studying abroad as well. Some states may require a master's degree after a certain amount of time on the job.

- *Performing arts/drama teachers:* In addition to the basic requirements to teach at the secondary education level, discussed previously, many states require that performing arts/drama teachers have a bachelor's degree in theater arts, as well as experience working in a community or professional theater setting.

As you can see, many—if not most—of these requirements vary by state. The best way to find out exactly what you need is to visit your state's department of education website or visit the websites of your perspective colleges to see what is expected and offered to specialist teachers.

Most states and school systems also require a criminal background clearance check in order to be able to teach. For example, to teach in Pennsylvania, prospective teachers must be cleared by the Department of Human Services Child Abuse History Clearance, the Pennsylvania State Police Request for Criminal Records Check, and the Federal Criminal History Record Information. Check with your state and potential school district for their requirements.

Experience-Related Requirements

This section covers the required experience to become a teacher, which is the student teaching you'll do during the course of your education. It also discusses other ways you can get experience in the educational field before and during the time you're pursuing your degree. This can and should start in middle school or high school, especially during the summers. Experience is important for many reasons, not the least:

- Shadowing others in the profession can help reveal what the job is really like and whether it's something that you think you want to do, day in and day out. This is a relatively risk-free way to explore different career paths. Ask any seasoned adult and he or she will tell you that figuring out what you *don't* want to do is sometimes more important than figuring out what you *do* want to do.
- Internships and volunteer work are a relatively quick way to gain work experience and develop job skills.

- Volunteering can help you learn the intricacies of the profession, such as what types of environments are best, what age of student fits you better, and which skills you need to work on.
- Gaining experience during your high school years sets you apart from the many others who are applying to programs.
- Volunteering at schools and other places means that you'll be meeting many others doing the job that you might someday want to do (think: career networking). You have the potential to develop mentor relationships, cultivate future job prospects, and get to know people who can recommend you for later positions. Studies show that about 85 percent of jobs are found through personal contacts.[6]

Experience can come in the form of being a camp counselor, tutoring kids, babysitting, being a lifeguard, working at the local YMCA, taking a cadet teaching class at school, finding a summer job that complements your subject matter interests, or even attending camps that foster your career aspirations. (See the TeenLife site at www.teenlife.com to start.) Consider these tidbits of advice to maximize your volunteer experience.[7] They will help you stand out:

- Get diverse experiences. For example, try to shadow at least two different teachers in different grade levels and schools.
- Try to gain forty hours of volunteer experience in each setting. This is typically considered enough to show that you understand what a full work week looks like in that setting. This can be as few as four to five hours per week over ten weeks or so.
- Find an aide/assistant/cadet position. Working as a paid assistant is by far the best experience you can get. This will prepare you nicely for your classroom experiences.
- Don't be afraid to ask questions. Just be considerate of the teachers' time and wait until they are not busy to pursue your questions. Asking good questions shows that you have a real curiosity for the profession.
- Maintain and cultivate professional relationships. Write thank-you notes, send updates about your application progress and tell them where you decide to go to school, and check in occasionally. If you want to find a good mentor, you need to be a gracious and willing mentee.

If you're interested in being a teacher, there's no such thing as too much
experience working with and mentoring kids.

GETTING EXPERIENCE IN THE CLASSROOM

If you're currently in high school and you're seriously thinking about becoming
a teacher, reach out to your favorite teachers or to a family friend who works
in a nearby school. Start by asking good questions and showing your curiosity. Ask to shadow the teachers, remembering the guidelines about courtesy

discussed above. Don't expect to be paid for any of this effort at first. The benefit of volunteering is that it's much easier to get your foot in the door, but the drawback is that you typically will not be paid. However, with time and hard work, your volunteer position may turn into something else.

"Take opportunities to get into a classroom and hang out and be an aide and work on projects with kids, so you can see what it's really like. Go to your counselor and ask about getting into a classroom—to start, just by observing. You can hang out with the kids and see what the class is like; that will help. Take the initiative to find schools that have a good education program and ask for help from your administration to get into those classrooms."—Karen Canning, seventh grade science teacher

---

Look at these kinds of experiences as ways to learn about the profession, show people how capable you are, and make connections with others that could last your career. It may even help you to get into the college of your choice, and it will definitely help you write your personal statement that explains why you want to be a teacher.

Another way to find a position—or at least a school district that is open to curious students—is to start with your high school guidance counselor or website, or visit the websites listed in this book. Don't be afraid to pick up the phone and call school offices. Be prepared to start by putting up bulletin boards, making copies, assisting teachers with clerical work, and other such tasks. Being on-site, no matter what you're doing, will teach you more than you know. With a great attitude and work ethic, you will likely be given more responsibility over time.

Once you are pursuing a degree in education, you will get many hours of hands-on teaching experience as well, but that will happen late in your college career. Don't wait until then to get into the classroom. However, the student teaching experience is very important to your growth as a teacher, and so it is discussed next.

MAKING THE MOST OF YOUR STUDENT-TEACHING EXPERIENCE

As mentioned earlier, the student-teaching experience is an important part of your education. It typically takes place during the last semester or year of your degree program. This is when you put everything you have learned—about your subject matter and about teaching—into practice. You get to test the waters of teaching in a classroom while supervised by an experienced teacher who will guide and mentor you. You will prepare lessons plans, manage the classroom, lead students, grade tests and assignments, solve problems, and more. During this experience you can begin to develop your own teaching style and focus on practicing the soft skills that are so important to teaching, such as:

- *Being flexible:* As much as you plan, things you don't anticipate will happen. You will learn to think on your feet.
- *Learning classroom management:* Managing a room full of students takes skill and lots of practice. It's a balance between keeping students on task and avoiding becoming a taskmaster.
- *Trying new and different ideas:* Now is the time to try some different ideas that you have. It's a safe environment to fail, and you might just spark some excitement and passion in your students!
- *Learning to show confidence in the classroom:* Being in command at the front of the room takes practice, too. You can really only master this by doing it, and you'll learn how to command respect from your students.

Be sure to ask for lots of feedback from your mentor teacher and from others. Don't be afraid to ask for advice from the entire teaching staff, and then be sure to have an open mind about the information you get back. You can become a better teacher through student teaching if you go into it with the best intentions.

Don't forget that once you are certified, you can work as a substitute teacher while you are looking for employment. This is a good way to get experience in a variety of settings and earn some money to pay the bills.

Networking

Because it's so important, another last word about networking. It's important to develop mentor relationships even at this stage. Remember that about 85 percent of jobs are found through personal contacts. If you know someone in the field, don't hesitate to reach out. Be patient and polite, but ask for help, perspective, and guidance.

> "Try to do any observing you can. Reach out to teachers who made an impact on your life; see if you can observe or shadow them. Even if it's a principal or admin that you got along with, reach out and make a connection so you can see what it's really like and what the teacher goes through."—Greg Wilson, seventh grade teacher

If you don't know anyone, ask your school guidance counselor to help you make connections. Or pick up the phone yourself. Reaching out with a genuine interest in knowledge and a real curiosity about the field will go a long way. You don't need a job or an internship just yet—just a connection that could blossom into a mentoring relationship. Follow these important but simple rules for the best results when networking:

- Do your homework about a potential contact, connection, university, school, or employer before you make contact. Be sure to have a general understanding of what they do and why. But don't be a know-it-all. Be open and ready to ask good questions.
- Be considerate of professionals' time and resources. Think about what they can get from you in return for mentoring or helping you.
- Speak and write using proper English. Proofread all your letters, e-mails, and even texts. Think about how you will be perceived at all times.
- Always stay positive.
- Show your passion for the kids and for the subject matter.

Don't forget that your high school guidance counselor can be a great source of information and connections as well.

Summary

In this chapter, you learned even more about what it's like to be a teacher. This chapter discussed the educational requirements of these different areas of teaching, from college degrees to licensing to master's degrees. You also learned about getting experience in the classroom and with kids in general, both before you enter college and during the educational process. At this time, you should have a good idea of the educational requirements of each area of teaching. You hopefully even contemplated some questions about what kind of educational career path fits your strengths, time requirements, and wallet. Are you starting to picture your career plan? If not, that's okay, as there's still time.

Remember that no matter which of these areas of teaching you pursue, you must maintain current certifications and meet continuing education requirements. This is very important in the education field. Advances in knowledge as well as changes in the pedagogy of teaching are continuous, and it's vitally important that you keep apprised of what's happening in your field. The bottom line is that you need to have a lifelong love of learning to succeed in education.

Chapter 3 goes into a lot more detail about pursing the best educational path. The chapter covers how to find the best value for your education and includes a discussion about financial aid and scholarships. At the end of chapter 3, you should have a much clearer view of the educational landscape and how and where you fit in.

3

Pursuing the Education Path

*W*hen it comes time to start looking at colleges, universities, or postsecondary schools, many high schoolers tend to freeze up at the enormity of the job ahead of them. This chapter will help break down this process for you so it won't seem so daunting.

It's true that finding the right college or learning institution is an important one, and it's a big step toward achieving your career goals and dreams. The last chapter covered the various educational requirements to become a teacher, which means you should now be ready to find the right institution of learning. This isn't always just a process of finding the very best school that you can afford and can be accepted into, although that might end up being your path. It should also be about finding the right fit so that you can have the best possible experience during your post–high school years.

But here's the truth of it all—attending postsecondary schooling isn't just about getting a degree. It's about learning how to be an adult, managing your life and your responsibilities, being exposed to new experiences, growing as a person, and otherwise moving toward becoming an adult who contributes to society. College offers you an opportunity to actually become an interesting person with perspective on the world and empathy and consideration for people other than yourself, if you let it.

An important component of how successful you will be in college is finding the right fit, the right school that brings out the best in you and challenges you at different levels. I know—no pressure, right? Just as with finding the right profession, your ultimate goal should be to match your personal interests, goals, and personality with the college's goals and perspective. For example, small liberal arts colleges have a much different feel and philosophy than Big 10 state schools. And rest assured that all this advice applies even if you're planning on attending community college or another postsecondary school.

Don't worry, though, in addition to these soft skills, this chapter does dive into the nitty-gritty of how to find the best school, no matter what you want to do. In the educational field specifically, attending a respected program is important to future success, and that is covered in detail in this chapter.

WHAT IS A GAP YEAR?

Taking a year off between high school and college, often called a gap year, is normal, perfectly acceptable, and almost required in many countries around the world. It is becoming increasingly acceptable in the United States as well. Even Malia Obama, President Obama's daughter, did it. Because the cost of college has gone up dramatically, it literally pays for you to know going in what you want to study, and a gap year—well spent—can do lots to help you answer that question.

Some great ways to spend your gap year include joining organizations such as the Peace Corps or AmeriCorps, enrolling in a mountaineering program or other gap year–styled program, backpacking across Europe or other countries on the cheap (be safe and bring a friend), finding a volunteer organization that furthers a cause you believe in or that complements your career aspirations, joining a Road Scholar program (see www.roadscholar.org), teaching English in another country (more information is available at www.gooverseas.com/blog/best-countries-for-seniors-to-teach-english -abroad), or working and earning money for college!

Many students will find that they get much more out of college when they have a year to mature and to experience the real world. The American Gap Year Association reports from alumni surveys that students who take gap years show greater civic engagement, higher college graduation rates, and higher grade point averages (GPAs) in college.[1]

You can use your gap year to explore and solidify your thoughts and plans about being a teacher while adding impressive experience to your college application. One caveat, though: If you aren't highly motivated to attend college, it can be somewhat dangerous to take a year off. Some kids tend to never return to school once they're away from it for a year. Be sure you have a plan and can stick to it if you're taking a year off.

See the association's website at https://gapyearassociation.org for lots of advice and resources if you're considering this potentially life-altering experience.

Finding a School That Fits Your Personality

Before looking at the details of good schools for teaching, it will behoove you to take some time to consider what type of school will be best for you. Answering questions like the ones that follow can help you narrow your search and focus on a smaller set of choices. Write your answers to these questions down somewhere where you can refer to them often, such as in the Notes app on your phone.

- *Size:* Does the size of the school matter to you? Colleges and universities range in size from five hundred or fewer students to twenty-five thousand students.
- *Community location:* Would you prefer to be in a rural area, a small town, a suburban area, or a large city? How important is the location of the school in the larger world?
- *Distance from home:* How far away from home—in terms of hours or miles away—do you want/are you willing to go?
- *Housing options:* What kind of housing would you prefer? Dorms, off-campus apartments, and private homes are all common options.
- *Student body:* How would you like the student body to look? Think about coed versus all-male and all-female settings, as well ethnic and racial diversity, how many students are part-time versus full-time, and the percentage of commuter students.
- *Academic environment:* Which majors are offered, and at which degree levels? Research the student-faculty ratio. Are the classes taught often by actual professors or more often by the teaching assistants? How many internships does the school typically provide to students? Are independent study or study abroad programs available in your area of interest?
- *Financial aid availability/cost:* Does the school provide ample opportunities for scholarships, grants, work-study programs, and the like? Does cost play a role in your options? (For most people, it does.)
- *Support services:* How strong are the school's academic and career placement counseling services?
- *Social activities and athletics:* Does the school offer clubs that you are interested in? Which sports are offered? Are scholarships available?
- *Specialized programs:* Does the school offer honors programs or programs for veterans or students with disabilities or special needs?

Not all of these questions are going to be important to you, and that's fine. Be sure to make note of aspects that don't matter as much to you. You might change your mind as you visit colleges, but it's important to make note of where you are to begin with.

Don't underestimate the value of the education you can get from your state university. Private schools can be double the cost and often do not specialize in education programs as in-depth as state schools, which traditionally produced teachers early in the twentieth century. State schools often tend to be the biggest bang for the buck in terms of a degree in education. Do your research!

U.S. News & World Report puts it best in reports that the college that fits you best is one that:

- Offers a degree that matches your interests and needs
- Provides a style of instruction that matches the way you like to learn
- Provides a level of academic rigor to match your aptitude and preparation
- Offers a community that feels like home to you
- Values you for what you do well[2]

Take some time to find the right academic fit; it's worth it.

According to the National Center for Educational Statistics, which is part of the US Department of Education, six years after entering college for an undergraduate degree, only 59 percent of students have graduated.[3] Barely half of those students will graduate from college in their lifetime.[4]

Hopefully, this section has impressed upon you the importance of finding the right college fit. Take some time to paint a mental picture of the kind of university or school setting that will best complement your needs. Then read on for specifics about teaching degrees.

TEACHING IS MENTORING

Jeff Hegnauer

Jeff Hegnauer has taught elementary education for twenty-one years, all at the same school in a large suburban school district. He has taught fourth grade for the past eleven years. He received his undergraduate degree in elementary education from Anderson University in 1998 and his master's degree in science education from Miami University in Ohio.

Can you explain how you became interested in being a teacher?

I have always been interested in working with kids. In high school, even, I was involved in study buddies, and I would go to the elementary schools to talk to students about drug and alcohol abuse prevention. I spent a few summers as a camp counselor, which piqued my interest in working with children. Also, I have always loved education and learning new things.

What is a typical day in your job?

[Laughs.] Well, there is no typical day in education, really. I get there about an hour to forty-five minutes before school begins and make sure I am prepared for the lessons. I greet students when they come in. This year, we are starting with writing right away, which we do for about an hour. They then go to their specials. Then we teach math for an hour and take the kids to lunch. I make any copies I need to make, eat my own lunch, and then join my students at recess for a game of kickball or foursquare or whatever they are playing. The afternoon is reading, science, and social studies. At 2:35, the kids leave. I get home by 4:30 or 5:00 usually. On Thursdays and Fridays, I prepare for the next week.

Tell me about student teachers that you've had in your class over the years.

I've had four student teachers and two cadet teachers from the high school in my twenty-one years of teaching. I enjoy really having them and mentoring them. It helps them see what it's really like all day, every day, and learn about classroom management. I highly recommend that kids who are interested in teaching get into the classroom.

What is the best part of your job?

The students, absolutely! Building relationships and seeing the growth with the kids from August to May is amazing. I help kids through struggles—most kids struggle with something. I find their strengths and build off of those. Helping them grow is very rewarding. The beauty of fourth grade, for example, is that they already know how to read, so we dig into the joy of reading and ask questions about the characters. What is the author's message, why do the characters do what they do, and why did the author make those choices? That's a lot of fun!

What is the most challenging part of your job?

Way too many people who have never been in a classroom have a lot of influence on what goes on in the classroom—the local-level administrators are great, but state government and beyond that can be challenging to deal with. It is even worse in other states from what I've heard. You often have to justify your methods, jump through hoops, etc.

Did your education prepare you for the job?

Coming out of undergrad, you are wide-eyed and all that, but I felt incredibly prepared with the pedagogy and background on kid psychology, i.e., how to learn and teach something. Not much can prepare you for how to deal with students and build those relationships. Being prepared for classroom management, etc., just takes practice, as well as how to build rapport with students. You just have to practice that.

In addition, I feel that my science master's degree really prepared me for scientific teaching. It was an amazing program, mostly online, and then I traveled in the summers and took courses in Costa Rica, Mexico, Trinidad, and Belize and did community-based conservation and scientific inquiry.

Why did you specifically pick elementary education?

I enjoy the age of kids in fourth to fifth grades especially. I also really like being more of a generalist. I got my master's in science education, which has been my favorite subject to teach. I really enjoy, personally, teaching everything. It's the kids but also about teaching everything. That's what drew me more to elementary education.

How can a young person who wants to be a teacher prepare for the experience?

High school students should get all the experience you can working with kids—get a job at the parks and recreation department or the local YMCA, summer camps, tutoring, etc. Get all the experience you can working with kids to learn how they tick and think. So you know if you enjoy it and can build rapport with students. Find something you really are passionate about to teach.

Has the job been what you expected?

Yes, it's been more than I expected or even dreamed. I knew I would enjoy it, but it grabbed hold of me. I can't picture ever doing anything else. There is something about teaching a subject matter that you love to someone else so they can engage with it that is amazing.

What would be your advice to a young person who is considering becoming a teacher?

Do it! It's the most amazing thing you can do. You get to spend 180 days with a great group of students. You see them change so much and accomplish so much. It's worth all the gray hairs and wrinkles. Enjoy it! You can make a difference in a kid's life.

If you don't have the passion or don't like students or the age group, don't do it. If you don't like kids, don't do it.

―――――――

Your Degree Plan for Studies in Education

The degree requirements to become a teacher in the United States vary depending on the grade level you want to teach, as well as whether you'll be teaching in public or private institutions. Here's a summary of the requirements for the two levels of teaching:

- *Elementary education (grades K–6):* All states require that kindergarten and elementary school teachers who teach in public schools have at least a bachelor's (four-year) degree. Private schools typically have this same requirement, but often set their own standards, so check with your school, if applicable. Some states also require public elementary education teachers to have certificates in a content area such as math or science. If you have not yet been to college, the best degree to pursue is a bachelor's in elementary education.

- *Secondary education (grades 7–12):* All states require that secondary education teachers who teach in public schools have at least a bachelor's (four-year) degree. Private schools typically have this same requirement. Most states require public high school teachers to have majored in the subject area they want to teach and also enrolled in their college's teacher preparation program, which usually includes classes in education and child psychology.[5]

In addition to a bachelor's degree, in some states and school districts you might be required to earn a master's degree after receiving your teaching certification and obtaining a job. Master's degree programs typically require two years of additional coursework. Even if a master's degree is not required in the state where you will be teaching, you will be required to attend continuing education classes and programs throughout your career as a teacher. Teachers also must complete yearly professional development classes in order to keep their license or certification active.

Transition-to-teaching programs facilitate the process of entering teaching and usually require only two semesters of coursework. Check out your state's department of education website for approved programs in your area. In addition, many states have fast-track certification programs for high-need areas such as STEM.

If you plan on teaching in a public school setting, you'll need to be licensed in the specific grade level in which you teach. (Teachers in private schools usually do not need a license.) The requirements to get a teacher's license vary by state, but they generally include:

The student teaching experience is a big part of the educational process for would-be teachers.

- A bachelor's degree with a certain minimum grade point average
- Completion of a teacher preparation program and supervised experience in teaching, which is typically through student teaching
- Passing a background check
- Passing a general teaching certification test, as well as a test that demonstrates knowledge of the subject you will teach[6]

SALARY DATA

Recall that the US Bureau of Labor Statistics reports that the average pay for teachers breaks down as follows: $56,900 (elementary); $57,720 (middle school); $59,190 (high school); and $59,980 (special education). Employment is expected to continue to grow 7–8 percent in the decade between 2016 and 2026, which is as fast as the average career.[7]

Keep in mind that these are averages across the country. If you live in the Midwest or the South, where the cost of living is lower, you'll likely make less than if you live on either coast. This is true regardless of profession. As an example, the average teacher in New York State makes about $75,000, whereas the average teacher in Oklahoma makes about $41,100. Check out the site www.teachersalaryinfo.com to see what teachers make in your area.

STARTING YOUR COLLEGE SEARCH

If you're currently in high school and you are serious about being a teacher, start by finding four to five schools in a realistic location (for you) that offer degrees in education. Not every school near you or that you have an initial interest in will offer an education degree, so narrow your choices accordingly. With that said, consider attending a public university in your resident state, if possible, which will save you lots of money. Private institutions don't typically discount resident student tuition costs.

Be sure you research the basic GPA and SAT or ACT requirements of each school as well.

For students applying to associate's degree programs or higher, most advisers recommend that students take both the ACT and the SAT during the spring of their junior year at the latest. (The ACT test is generally considered more heavily weighted in science, so take that into consideration.) You can retake these tests and use your highest score, so be sure to leave time for a retake early in your senior year if needed. You want your best score to be available to all the schools you're applying to by January of your senior year, which will also enable your score to be considered with any scholarship applications. Keep in mind that these are general timelines—be sure to check the exact deadlines and calendars of the schools to which you're applying!

Once you have found four to five schools in a realistic location for you that offer the degree you want to pursue, spend some time on their websites studying the requirements for admission. Most universities list the average stats for the last class accepted to the program. Important factors in your decision about what schools to apply to should include whether or not you meet the requirements, your chances of getting in (but shoot high!), tuition costs and availability of scholarships and grants, location, and the school's reputation and licensure/graduation rates.

The importance of these characteristics will depend on your grades and test scores, your financial resources, and other personal factors. You want to find a university with a good education program that also matches your academic rigor and practical needs.

FINDING THE RIGHT SCHOOL

Finding the university or college that's best for you is going to depend on lots of personal factors, as mentioned in the previous sections. However, there are a few facts about the school's education program that you can find out and compare across the board with other schools, such as:

- How much time do college students spend student teaching/in the classroom, and when do supervised teaching experiences begin?
- Is the school accredited, and by whom? Education programs are typically accredited by Council for the Accreditation of Educator Preparation and/or the Higher Learning Commission.
- What are the attrition rates (the number of students who leave the program without graduating)?
- What percentage of last year's graduates are employed as teachers?
- How is the education school ranked in the nation?

These factors, combined with the others mentioned in this chapter, should help you get a holistic view of each college you're considering. In all likelihood, no single factor will determine your best choice. Consider making a grid with all these factors mapped out for each school. Sometimes it's helpful to get everything down on paper and take a look at it all together in one place.

THE MOST PERSONAL OF PERSONAL STATEMENTS

The personal statement you include with your application to college is extremely important, especially if your GPA and SAT/ACT scores are on the border of what is typically accepted. Write something that is thoughtful and conveys your understanding of the education profession, as well as your desire to be a teacher. Why are you uniquely qualified? Why are you a good fit for the university and program or these types of students? These essays should be highly personal (the "personal" in personal statement). Will the admissions professionals who read it—along with hundreds of others—come away with a snapshot of who you really are and what you are passionate about?

Look online for some examples of good personal statements, which will give you a feel for what works. Be sure to check your specific school for length guidelines, format requirements, and any other guidelines you are expected to follow. Most important, make sure your passion for teaching, for children, and for the subject you'll teach comes through in your personal statement.

And of course, be sure to proofread it several times and ask a professional (such as your school writing center or your local library services) to proofread it as well.

What's It Going to Cost You?

So, the bottom line: what will your education end up costing you? Of course, this depends on many factors, including the type and length of degree you pursue, where you attend (in-state or not, private or public institution), how much in scholarships or financial aid you're able to obtain, your family or personal income, and many other factors. The College Entrance Examination Board tracks and summarizes financial data from colleges and universities all over the United States. (You can find more information at www.collegeboard.org.) A sample of the most recent data is shown in table 3.1.

Table 3.1. Average Yearly Tuition, Fees, Room, and Board for Full-Time Undergraduates (Published Prices)

Year	Public 2-Year	Public 4-Year, In-State	Public 4-Year, Out-of-State	Private Nonprofit
2016–2017	$11,640	$20,150	$35,300	$45,370
2017–2018	$11,970	$20,770	$36,420	$46,950

Source: College Entrance Examination Board website, https://parents.collegeboard.org/faq/how-much-tuition

Keep in mind that these are averages and reflect the published prices, not the net prices (see the sidebar "The All-Important Net Cost"). If you read more specific data about a particular university or find averages in your particular area of interest, you should assume those numbers are closer to reality than these, as they are more specific. This data helps to show you the ballpark figures.

THE ALL-IMPORTANT NET COST

The actual, final price (or net price) that you'll pay for a specific college is the published price (tuition and fees) to attend that college, minus any grants, scholarships, and education tax benefits you receive (money you don't have to pay back). This difference can be significant. In 2015–2016, the average published price of in-state tuition and fees for public four-year colleges was about $9,139 (*not* including room and board), but the average net price of in-state tuition and fees for public four-year colleges was only about $3,030.[8]

Most college websites have net price calculators on their websites that use the information you enter to come up with a personalized estimate of how much gift aid that particular college may offer you—and consequently what it will really cost you to attend. (So the net price is a personal number that varies from student to student. It considers factors like financial need, academic performance, and athletic talent.) The net price is the best number to use when you're comparing different university costs, because it takes into account each school's scholarships and grants, which can vary significantly from school to school. By comparing net prices instead of the published prices, you might find out that you can actually afford the school you thought was too expensive!

Generally speaking, there is about a 3 percent annual increase in tuition and associated costs to attend college. In other words, if you are expecting to attend college two years after this data was collected, you need to add approximately 6 percent to these numbers. Keep in mind that this assumes no financial aid or scholarships of any kind (so it's not the net cost).

This chapter discusses finding the most affordable path to get the degree you want. Later in this chapter, you'll also learn how to prime the pumps and get as much money for college as you can.

Touring the campus and talking to current students is really important.

MAKE THE MOST OF SCHOOL VISITS

If it's at all practical and feasible, you should visit the schools you're considering. To get a real feel for any college or school, you need to walk around the campus and buildings, spend some time in the common areas where students hang out, and sit in on a few classes. You can also sign up for campus tours, which are typically given by current students. This is another good way to see the school and ask questions of someone who knows. Be sure to visit the specific school/building that covers your intended major as well. Websites and brochures won't be able to convey that intangible feeling you'll get from a visit.

Make a list of questions that are important to you before you visit. In addition to the questions listed earlier in this chapter, consider these questions as well:

- What is the makeup of the current freshman class? Is the campus diverse?
- What is the meal plan like? What are the food options?
- Where do most of the students hang out between classes? (Be sure to visit this area.)
- How long does it take to walk from one end of campus to the other?
- What types of transportation are available for students? Does campus security provide escorts to cars, dorms, and other on-campus destinations at night?

To prepare for your visit and make the most of it, consider these tips and words of advice:

- Be sure to do some research. At the very least, spend some time on the college's website. You may find your questions are addressed adequately there.
- Make a list of questions.
- Arrange to meet with a professor in your area of interest or to visit the specific school.
- Be prepared to answer questions about yourself and why you are interested in this school.
- Dress in neat, clean, and casual clothes. Avoid overly wrinkled clothing or anything with stains.
- Listen and take notes.

- Don't interrupt.
- Be positive and energetic.
- Make eye contact when someone speaks directly to you.
- Ask questions.
- Thank people for their time.

Finally, be sure to send thank-you notes or e-mails after the visit is over. Remind recipients when you visited the campus and thank them for their time.

Financial Aid and Student Loans

Finding the money to attend college—whether a two- or four-year college program, an online program, or a vocational career college—can seem overwhelming. But you can do it if you have a plan before you actually start applying to colleges. If you get into your top-choice university, don't let the sticker price turn you away. Financial aid can come from many different sources, and it's available to cover all different kinds of costs you'll encounter during your years in college, including tuition, fees, books, housing, and food.

Paying for college can take a creative mix of grants, scholarships, and loans, but you can find your way with some help!

The good news is that universities more often offer incentive or tuition discount aid to encourage students to attend. The market is often more competitive in the favor of the student, and colleges and universities are responding by offering more generous aid packages to a wider range of students than they used to. Here are some basic tips and pointers about the financial aid process:

- Apply for financial aid during your senior year. You must fill out the Free Application for Federal Student Aid (FAFSA) form, which can be filed starting October 1 of your senior year until June of the year you graduate.[9] Because the amount of available aid is limited, it's best to apply as soon as you possibly can. See https://studentaid.ed.gov/sa/fafsa to get started.
- Be sure to compare and contrast the deals you get from different schools. There is room to negotiate with universities. The first offer for aid may not be the best you'll get.
- Wait until you receive all offers from your top schools and then use this information to negotiate with your top choice to see if they will match or beat the best aid package you received.
- To be eligible to keep and maintain your financial aid package, you must meet certain grade/GPA requirements. Be sure you are very clear about these academic expectations and keep up with them.
- You must reapply for federal aid every year.

Watch out for scholarship scams! You should never be asked to pay to submit the FAFSA form (*free* is in its name) or be required to pay a lot to find appropriate aid and scholarships. These are free services. If an organization promises you you'll get aid or that you have to "act now or miss out," these are warning signs of a less-than-reputable organization.

You should also be careful with your personal information to avoid identity theft as well. Simple things like closing and exiting your browser after visiting sites where you entered personal information goes a long way. Don't share your student aid ID number with anyone, either.

It's important to understand the different forms of financial aid that are available to you. That way, you'll know how to apply for different kinds and get the best financial aid package that fits your needs and strengths. The two main categories that financial aid falls under are gift aid, which doesn't have to be repaid, and self-help aid, which includes loans that must be repaid and work-study funds that are earned. The next sections cover the various types of financial aid that fit into these areas.

GRANTS

Grants typically are awarded to students who have financial need, but can also be used in the areas of athletics, academics, demographics, veteran support, and special talents. They do not have to be paid back. Grants can come from federal agencies, state agencies, specific universities, and private organizations. Most federal and state grants are based on financial need.

Examples of grants are the Pell Grant, SMART Grant, TEACH grant (see the sidebar for more information), and Federal Supplemental Educational Opportunity Grant. Visit the US Department of Education's Federal Student Aid site at https://studentaid.ed.gov/types/grants-scholarships for lots of current information about grants.

WHAT IS THE TEACH GRANT?

Offered by the federal government through the US Department of Education, he TEACH Grant provides up to $4,000 a year to students who are completing the coursework needed to begin a career in teaching. In return, recipients agree to fulfill a service obligation; failure to fulfill that obligation converts the grant to a direct unsubsidized loan, which means you must pay it back with interest.

In exchange for receiving a TEACH Grant, you must agree specifically to the following:

- You must serve as a full-time teacher for a total of at least four academic years within eight years after you complete or otherwise cease to be enrolled in the program for which you received TEACH Grant funds.
- You must perform the teaching service at a low-income school or educational service agency, as defined by the US Department of Education. These include elementary or secondary schools operated by the US Department of the Interior's Bureau of Indian Education (BIE) or operated on reservations by tribal groups under contract or grant with the BIE.

- Your teaching service must be in a high-need field. These fields include bilingual education and English language acquisition, foreign language, mathematics, reading specialists, science, and special education.

If you are willing to teach in less-served areas and serve your community and country in this way, you can earn a lot of money in grants in exchange for your service. See https://studentaid.ed.gov/sa/types/grants-scholarships/teach for more information about the requirements, what kinds of schools qualify, and how to apply.

SCHOLARSHIPS

Scholarships are merit-based aid that does not have to be paid back. They are typically awarded based on academic excellence or some other special talent, such as music or art. Scholarships can also be athletic-based, minority-based, aid for women, and so forth. These are typically not awarded by federal or state governments, but instead come from the specific school you applied to as well as private and nonprofit organizations.

Be sure to reach out directly to the financial aid officers of the schools you want to attend. These people are great contacts who can lead you to many more sources of scholarships and financial aid. Visit GoCollege's Financial Aid Finder at www.gocollege.com/financial-aid/scholarships/types for lots more information about how scholarships in general work.

LOANS

Many types of loans are available especially for students to pay for their post-secondary education. However, the important thing to remember here is that loans must be paid back, with interest. (This is the extra cost of borrowing the money and is usually a percentage of the amount you borrow.) Be sure you understand the interest rate you will be charged. Is this fixed or will it change over time? Are payments on the loan and interest deferred until you graduate (meaning you don't have to begin paying it off until after you graduate)? Is the loan subsidized (meaning the federal government pays the interest until you graduate)? These are all points you need to be clear about before you sign on the dotted line.

There are many types of loans offered to students, including need-based loans, non-need-based loans, state loans, and private loans. Two very reputable federal loans are the Perkins Loan and the Direct Stafford Loan. For more information about student loans, visit https://bigfuture.collegeboard.org/pay -for-college/loans/types-of-college-loans.

FEDERAL WORK-STUDY

The US federal work-study program provides part-time jobs for undergraduate and graduate students with financial need so they can earn money to pay for educational expenses. The focus of such work is on community service work and work related to a student's course of study. Not all schools participate in this program, so be sure to check with the financial aid office at any schools you are considering if this is something you are counting on. The sooner you apply, the more likely you will get the job you desire and be able to benefit from the program, as funds are limited. See https://studentaid.ed.gov/sa/types/work -study for more information about this opportunity.

DON'T FORGET TO TEACH WITH CREATIVITY AND COMPASSION

Denise Cotton

Denise Cotton graduated from Purdue University with a bachelor's degree in biology and a minor in education. After teaching one year in middle school, her life circumstances changed and she worked for a pharmaceutical company as a bio-chemist for ten years. After raising her kids and being out of the full-time job market for about twenty years, she took a job teaching chemistry at a local high school and has been teaching for about ten years.

Can you explain how you became interested in being a teacher and the specific educational process you went through?

I started off in middle school, teaching one year. Then we moved and I got a job in industry, at Eli Lilly. I worked there as a biochemist doing insulin purification for ten years. The kind of stuff I did there actually did have a teaching aspect to it. I had to connect the science to the production floor employees, which involved teaching. Teaching is interpreting in a way, and part of my job was to interpret the science for these employees. I enjoyed the teaching aspect of that job a lot.

I then had children and stopped working full-time for about twenty years. In 2008, I wanted to begin working again, and teaching really appealed to me. I began teaching at a large suburban high school. I teach regular and honors chemistry, mostly to sophomores and juniors.

What is a typical day in your job?

I don't stop working the whole day! I arrive at school at about 6:15 (an hour before the students). I get the labs set up and make copies. I plan things, grade papers, and so on. I teach two different courses—honors and regular chemistry—in five different classes during one semester. So I have about 130 students total each semester.

The school day is 7:20 a.m.–2:35 p.m. So during that day, I have five classes of chemistry students, a study hall to supervise, twenty-five minutes for lunch, and a forty-five-minute prep period. During the prep time, I take care of anything that involves leaving the classroom, such as making copies, getting chemicals, talking to other teachers, using the computer to create presentations, creating tests, grading, and so on.

Three afternoons a week we have meetings after school. Some are for professional development (training on giving standardized tests, how not to be biased, and so on), some are faculty meetings, and some are teacher meetings. I get home about 4:00–4:30.

I frequently take work home; intensive work—like developing a whole new unit, for example—I prefer to do at home. I feel like the work is never done—there are always improvements that you could be making to your job. You have to try to not go stale and continue to improve. Kids know if you're interested in your subject content—even if they aren't! If you are bored, how can they be interested?

Why did you choose secondary education and then the high school setting?

I am academically oriented and enjoy the depth of content you get at the high school level. I really like the chemistry and biology at the level I teach it. I enjoy teaching something that's challenging. I try to treat the students as adults, and they often rise to the occasion. I like the idea that they can take responsibility for their own learning. They don't always do it, but it's good to set those expectations. It's a better fit for my personality.

What is the best part of your job?

I really like planning something and then seeing it work. I love seeing the students understand, learn, and like it! When the students like it *and* it's cool *and* they get the idea as well, it's great. I like being around high school kids, but it's different than parenting. You can enjoy chatting with them but aren't responsible for their lives. I also enjoy the relationships with other teachers. In my experience, teachers are not territorial and are always willing to help each other out. We are always there to help each other and share ideas and lesson plans with each other.

Another great thing about teaching is that the job starts completely over every year. There is a lot of room to be creative, which I love. I love being creative in how I will communicate a concept—getting away from the lecture/presentation format when I can. Developing hands-on and interactive stuff to help with learning, such as YouTube, stations around the room, etc. A good teacher plans for different kinds of learners and tries to hit everyone's strengths and maximizes the interaction in the room. Students helping students is great, too. That's one of the fun things about teaching—always trying new things and getting better.

What is the most challenging part of your job?

You don't know your students as well as you would at the elementary school level. The challenging part of this is that you don't know what's going on in their lives. Studies show that one out of five teens is clinically depressed and many go undiagnosed. That means I have five or six students in my classes who are depressed or have other serious challenges that I don't know about. I really don't know what's going on in their lives. That's just the way it is. You can't be super rigid and you have to teach with compassion. A lot of teachers coach or have a club that they supervise, which is a great way to develop deeper relationships with students. It's a step beyond the relationship in the classroom.

Also, there are students who don't want to work or learn. You can try to motivate them, but ultimately it's up to them. They aren't willing or able to put forth the effort to succeed, and that's frustrating to see as a teacher.

Did your education prepare you for the job?

It certainly prepared me for the content portion of the job. Any teacher will tell you that there really is no substitute for on-the-job learning.

How can a young person who wants to be a teacher prepare for the experience?

Find and take the cadet teaching program offered at your high school to assist in your local school district—a period or two out of the day where you leave the high school and assist at a local school. It's a class that's offered at the high school. Try being a camp counselor, working at the YMCA, and working with young groups whenever you can.

Has the job been what you expected and how has it changed?

I have evolved over time, and the technology changes have also been considerable. There is a positive and negative aspect to technology. Online quizzes and Canvas and assignments online, working collaboratively—those are all good. The negative aspect is the distraction of phones and the general need students feel to be entertained. You have to work much harder as a teacher to create entertaining and engaging modules. Everything needs to be entertaining and interactive, even when it's not the best approach. I don't really think kids have changed fundamentally. Kids are kids. Maybe they have lower attention spans and are less willing to slug their way through something difficult (less grit). They might give up more easily and ask for help, a product of the Google generation.

What would be your advice to a young person who is considering becoming a teacher?

Get as much experience with kids at the level you're considering and make sure you like it. Get experience before you commit to getting a teaching degree. You don't want to invest all the time, money, and education and then, after a year or two, decide that you hate it. The best programs get students into the classrooms right away. Teaching doesn't pay great—but do what you love, not for the money. Do a job that you love and hope that it pays the bills.

Talk to your favorite teachers at different levels and ask them their story. Consider the different settings, too, and which is good for you, culturally and so on.

═══════════════

Making High School Count

If you are still in high school or middle school, there are many things you can do now to help the postsecondary educational process go more smoothly. Consider these tips for your remaining years:

- Work on listening well and speaking and communicating clearly. Work on writing clearly and effectively.
- Learn how to learn. This means keeping an open mind, asking questions, asking for help when you need it, taking good notes, and doing your homework.
- Plan a daily homework schedule and keep up with it. Have a consistent, quiet place to study.

- Talk about your career interests with friends, family, and counselors. They may have connections to people in your community who you can shadow or who will mentor you.
- Try new interests and activities, especially during your first two years of high school.
- Be involved in extracurricular activities that truly interest you and say something about who you are and who you want to be.

Kids are under so much pressure these days to do it all, but you should think about working smarter rather than harder. If you are involved in things you enjoy, your educational load won't seem like such a burden. Be sure to take time for self-care, such as sleep, unscheduled down time, and activities that you find fun and energizing. See chapter 4 for more ways to relieve and avoid stress.

Summary

This chapter looked at all the aspects of college and postsecondary schooling that you'll want to consider as you move forward. Remember that finding the right fit is especially important, as it increases the chances that you'll stay in school and finish your degree or program—and have an amazing experience while you're there.

In this chapter, you learned about how to get the best education for the best deal. You also learned a little about scholarships and financial aid, how the SAT and ACT tests work, and how to write a unique personal statement that eloquently expresses your passions.

Use this chapter as a jumping-off point to dig deeper into your particular area of interest, but don't forget these important points:

- Take the SAT and ACT tests early in your junior year so you have time to take them again if you need to. Most schools automatically accept the highest scores.
- Make sure that the school you plan to attend has an accredited program in your field of study. This is particularly important in fields that use federal funds, like teaching. Some schools follow national policies, while others use state-mandated policies and therefore differ across state lines. Do your research and understand the differences.

- Don't underestimate how important school visits are, especially in the pursuit of finding the right academic fit. Come prepared to ask questions not addressed on the school's website or in the literature.
- Your personal statement is a very important piece of your application that can set you apart from other applicants. Take the time and energy needed to make it unique and compelling.
- Don't assume you can't afford a school based on the sticker price. Many schools offer great scholarships and aid to qualified students. It doesn't hurt to apply. This advice especially applies to minorities, veterans, and students with disabilities.
- Don't lose sight of the fact that it's important to pursue a career that you enjoy, are good at, and are passionate about! You'll be a happier person if you do so—and so will your students.

At this point, your career goals and aspirations should be jelling. At the very least, you should have a plan for finding out more information. And don't forget about networking, which was covered in more detail in chapter 2. Remember to do research about the school or degree program before you reach out and especially before you visit. Faculty and staff find students who ask challenging questions much more impressive than those who ask questions that can be answered by spending ten minutes on the school's website.

Chapter 4 goes into detail about the next steps—writing a résumé and cover letter, interviewing well, follow-up communications, and more. This information is not just for college grads; you can use it to secure internships, volunteer positions, summer jobs, and other opportunities. In fact, the sooner you can hone these communication skills, the better off you'll be in the professional world.

4

Writing Your Résumé and Interviewing

No matter which kind of teacher you aspire to be, having a well-written résumé and impeccable interviewing skills will help you reach your ultimate goals. This chapter provides some helpful tips and advice to build the best résumé and cover letter, how to interview well with prospective employers, and how to communicate effectively and professionally at all times. The advice in this chapter isn't just for people entering the workforce full-time, either; it can help you score that internship or summer job or help you give a great college interview to impress the admissions office.

After discussing how to write your résumé, the chapter looks at important interviewing skills that you can build and develop over time. The chapter also has some tips for dealing successfully with stress, which is an inevitable by-product of a busy life.

Writing Your Résumé

If you're a teen writing a résumé for your first job, you likely don't have a lot of work experience under your belt yet. Because of this limited work experience, you need to include classes and coursework that are related to the job you're seeking, as well as any school activities and volunteer experience you have. While you are writing your résumé, you might discover some talents and recall some activities you did that you forgot about but that are important to add. Think about volunteer work, side jobs you've held (babysitting, being a camp counselor, tutoring, dog walking, etc.), and the like. A good approach at this point in your career is to build a functional résumé, which focuses on your abilities rather than work experience, and it's discussed in detail next.

PARTS OF A RÉSUMÉ

The functional résumé is the best approach when you don't have a lot of pertinent work experience, as it is written to highlight your abilities rather than your experience. (The other, perhaps more common, type of résumé is called the chronological résumé, which lists a person's accomplishments in chronological order, most recent jobs listed first.) This section breaks down and discusses the functional résumé in greater detail.

Here are the essential parts of your résumé, listed from the top down:

- *Heading:* This should include your name, address, and contact information, including phone, e-mail, and website if you have one. This information is typically centered at the top of the page.
- *Objective:* This is one-sentence that tells the employer what kind of position you are seeking. This should be modified to be specific to each potential employer.
- *Education:* Always list your most recent school or program first. Include date of completion (or expected date of graduation), degree or certificate earned, and the institution's name and address. Include workshops, seminars, and related classes here as well.
- *Skills:* Skills include computer literacy, leadership skills, organizational skills, and time-management skills. Be specific in this area when possible, and tie your skills to working with kids when it's appropriate.
- *Activities:* Activities can be related to skills. Perhaps an activity listed here helped you develop a skill listed above. This section can be combined with the Skills section, but it's often helpful to break these apart if you have enough substantive things to say in both areas. Examples include camps, sports teams, leadership roles, community service work, clubs and organizations, and so on, as well as any activities that involved working with and mentoring kids.
- *Experience:* If you don't have any actual work experience that's relevant, you might consider skipping this section. However, you can list summer, part-time, and volunteer jobs you've held, again focusing on work with children.
- *Interests:* This section is optional, but it's a chance to include special talents and interests. Keep it short, factual, and specific.
- *References:* It's best to say that references are available on request. If you do list actual contacts, list no more than three and make sure you inform your contacts that they might be contacted.

The first three parts above are pretty much standard, but the others can be creatively combined or developed to maximize your abilities and experience. These are not set-in-stone sections that every résumé must have.

RÉSUMÉ-WRITING TIPS FOR TEACHERS

The best résumé for scoring a teaching position is one that highlights your education (and credentials, if you have any yet). Teaching jobs usually require specific degrees and certifications, so make sure to include an "Education" section toward the top of your résumé.

Be sure to include all teaching-related experience. Especially if you're just starting out, this includes volunteer positions in any classroom setting (e.g., cadet teaching, teacher assisting) as well as activities that involve teaching or working with kids in some way, such as being a camp counselor, babysitting, tutoring, or working as a lifeguard. Many summer jobs can be marketed as "working with kids," but always be genuine and honest.

Modify each résumé and cover letter to the job you're applying for. Be sure to highlight different aspects of your experience depending on the specific requirements of the position you're applying for. One way to do that is to include keywords from the job listing in your résumé. Look for important words in the job listing (such as particular qualifications, skills, etc.) and try to include them in your résumé to demonstrate that you are a good fit for the job—but again, always be honest about your skills and accomplishments.

Note that most applications for education positions must be done online at the employer's website, with the résumé included as an attachment. In these applications, cover letters are often optional.

If you're still not seeing the big picture here, it's helpful to look at student and part-time résumé examples online to see how others have approached this process. Search for "functional résumé examples" to get a look at some examples.

RÉSUMÉ-WRITING TIPS

Regardless of your situation and why you're writing the résumé, there are some basic tips and techniques you should use:

- Keep it short and simple. This includes using a simple, standard font and format. Using one of the résumé templates included in your word processor software can be a great way to start.
- Use simple language. Keep it to one page.
- Highlight your academic achievements, such as a high GPA (above 3.5) or academic awards. If you have taken classes related to the job you're interviewing for, list those briefly as well.
- Emphasize your extracurricular activities, internships, and the like. These could include camps, clubs, sports, babysitting, tutoring, or volunteer work. Use these activities to show your skills, interests, and abilities.
- Use action verbs, such as *led, created, taught, ran,* and *developed.*
- Be specific and give examples.
- Always be honest.
- Include leadership roles and experience.
- Edit and proofread at least twice, and have someone else do the same. Ask a professional (such as your school writing center or your local library services) to proofread it for you also. Don't forget to run spell check.
- Include a cover letter (discussed in the next section).

THE COVER LETTER

Every résumé you send out should include a cover letter, with some exceptions dealing with online applications. It's best to check the individual school's requirements before you submit your materials. This can be the most important part of your job search because it's often the first thing that potential employers read. By including the cover letter, you're showing the school that you took the time to learn about their organization and address them personally. This goes a long way to show that you're interested in the position.

Be sure to call the school corporation or verify on the website the name and title of the person to whom you should address the letter. This letter should be brief. Introduce yourself and begin with a statement that will grab the person's attention. Keep in mind that employers potentially receive hundreds of résumés and cover letters for every open position. You want yours to stand out. Important information to include in the cover letter, from the top, includes:

- The current date
- Your address and contact information
- The person's name, school, and contact information

Then you begin the letter portion of the cover letter, which should mention how you heard about the position, something extra about you that will interest the potential employer, practical skills you can bring to the position, and past experience related to the job. You should apply the facts outlined in your résumé to the job to which you're applying. Each cover letter should be personalized for the position and school corporation to which you're applying. Don't use "To whom it may concern"; instead, take the time to find out to whom you should actually address the letter. Finally, end with a complimentary closing, such as "Sincerely, Christopher E. Smith," and be sure to add your signature. Search for "sample cover letters for internships" or "sample cover letters for high schoolers" to see some good examples. Consider this mock cover letter as an example.

Christopher Endsley Smith
120 Cherry Street
Portland, OR 97035

September 2, 2024

Ms. Patricia Jones
Superintendent
Kermit United School District
511 W 10th Ave.
Portland, OR 97035

Dear Ms. Jones,

I'm writing based on an article I read in the July 9th edition of the *Portland Star*, where you described the Kermit School District as "one with heart and passion". As a student focusing on a career in special education, that phrase jumped off the page at me. Without heart and passion, why would anyone teach?

I believe my experience working with kids with special needs during my summers in high school and my current focus on special education studies meld well with your mission. As you can see from my enclosed resume, I have been fortunate to spend over 50 hours in service to kids with special needs. In addition to my camp experience, for the past two years, I've served as a part-time tutor for special needs' students. This has solidified my determination and desire to teach in this area.

I'm ready to use my skills and passions in a formal educational environment, which is my career goal. I'm believe I am very good at understanding children with special needs and communicating with them. I look forward to furthering my knowledge and experience, which I believe I can do in the Kermit school district, to the benefit of us both.

Please see my resume for additional information about my studies and coursework. I can be reached anytime on my cellphone at 555-555-5555.

Thank you for your time and consideration.

Sincerely,

Christopher Smith

Christopher E. Smith

Your cover letter can be the most important part of your job search
because it's often the first thing potential employers see.

If you are e-mailing your cover letter instead of printing it out, you'll need to pay particular attention to the subject line of your e-mail. Be sure that it is specific to the position you are applying for. In all cases, it's really important to follow the employer's instructions about how to submit your cover letter and résumé. Generally speaking, sending PDFs rather than editable documents is a better idea. Everyone can read a PDF, but some recipients might not be able to open a document from the particular word-processing program that you used. Most word-processing programs have an option under the Save command that allows you to save your document as a PDF.

EFFECTIVELY HANDLING STRESS

As you're forging ahead with your life plans—whether it's college, working full-time as a teaching assistant, or even a gap year—you might find that these decisions feel very important and heavy and that the stress is difficult to deal with. This is completely normal. Try these simple techniques to relieve stress:

- Take deep breaths in and out. Try this for thirty seconds. You'll be amazed at how it can help.
- Close your eyes and clear your mind.
- Go scream at the passing subway car. Or lock yourself in a closet and scream. Or scream into a pillow. For some people, this can really help.
- Keep the issue in perspective. Any decision you make now can be changed if it doesn't work out.

Want to know how to avoid stress altogether? It is surprisingly simple. Of course, simple doesn't always mean easy, but these ideas are basic and make sense based on what we know about the human body:

- Get enough sleep.
- Eat healthy.
- Get exercise.
- Go outside.
- Schedule downtime.
- Connect with friends and family.

The bottom line is that you need to take time for self-care. There will always be conflict, but how you deal with it makes all the difference. This only becomes more important as you enter college or the workforce and maybe have a family. Developing good, consistent habits related to self-care now will serve you all your life.

Interviewing Skills

The best way to avoid nerves and keep calm when you're interviewing is to be prepared. It's okay to feel scared, but keep it in perspective. It's likely that you'll receive many more rejections than acceptances in your professional life, as we all do. However, you only need one *yes* to start out. Think of the interviewing process as a learning experience. With the right attitude, you will learn from each one and get better with each subsequent interview. That should be your overarching goal. Consider these tips and tricks when interviewing, whether it be for a teaching job, internship, college admission, or something else entirely:

- Practice interviewing with a friend or relative. Practicing will help calm your nerves and make you feel more prepared. Ask for specific feedback from your friends. Do you need to speak more loudly? Are you making enough eye contact? Are you actively listening when the other person is speaking?
- Learn as much as you can about the company, school, or organization, and be sure to understand the position for which you're applying. This will show the interviewer that you are motivated and interested in their organization.
- Speak up during the interview. Convey to the interviewer important points about yourself. Don't be afraid to ask questions. Try to remember the interviewers' names and call them by name.
- Arrive early and dress professionally and appropriately. (You can read more about proper dress in a following section.)
- Take some time to prepare answers to commonly asked questions. Be ready to describe your career or educational goals to the interviewer.[1]

Common questions you may be asked during a job interview include:

- Tell me about yourself.
- What are your greatest strengths?
- What are your weaknesses?
- Why do you want to work with children?
- Tell me something about yourself that's not on your résumé.
- What are your career goals?
- How do you handle failure? Are you willing to fail?
- How do you handle stress and pressure?
- What are you passionate about?
- Why do you want to work for us?

Common questions you may be asked during a college admissions interview include:

- Tell me about yourself.
- Why are you interested in going to college?
- Why do you want to major in this subject?
- What are your academic strengths?
- What are your academic weaknesses? How have you addressed them?
- What will you contribute to this college/school/university?
- Where do you see yourself in ten years?
- How do you handle failure? Are you willing to fail?
- How do you handle stress and pressure?
- Whom do you most admire?
- What is your favorite book?
- What do you do for fun?
- Why are you interested in this college/school/university?

Jot down notes about your answers to these questions, but don't try to memorize the answers. You don't want to come off as too rehearsed during the interview. Remember to be as specific and detailed as possible when answering these questions. Your goal is to set yourself apart in some way from the other interviewees. Always accentuate the positive, even when you're asked about something you did not like, or about failure or stress. Most importantly, though, be yourself.

Active listening is the process of fully concentrating on what is being said, understanding it, and providing nonverbal cues and responses to the person talking.[2] It's the opposite of being distracted and thinking about something else when someone is talking. Active listening takes practice. You might find that your mind wanders and you need to bring your attention back to the person talking (and this could happen multiple times during one conversation). Practice this technique in regular conversations with friends and relatives. In addition to giving a better interview, it can cut down on nerves and make you more popular with friends and family, as everyone wants to feel that they are really being heard. For more on active listening, check out www.mindtools.com/CommSkll/ActiveListening.htm.

You should also be ready to ask questions of your interviewer. In a practical sense, there should be some questions you have that you can't find the answer to on the website or in the literature. Also, asking questions shows that you are interested and have done your homework. Avoid asking questions about salary, scholarships, or special benefits at this stage, and don't ask about anything negative you've heard about the company or school. Keep the questions positive and related to the position to which you're applying. Some example questions to potential employers include:

- What is a typical career path for a person in this position?
- How would you describe the ideal candidate for this position?
- How long, on the average, does a teacher stay at this school?
- How is the department organized?
- What kind of responsibilities come with this job? (Don't ask this if it has already been addressed in the job description or discussion.)
- What can I do as a follow-up?
- When do you expect to reach a decision?

See "Make the Most of Campus Visits" in chapter 3 for some good examples of questions to ask the college admissions office. The important thing is to write your own questions related to information you really want to know, and be sure your question isn't already answered on the website, in the job description, or in the literature. This will show genuine interest.

Dressing Appropriately

It's important to determine what is actually appropriate in the setting of the interview. What is appropriate in a corporate setting might be different from what you'd expect at a small liberal arts college or at a large hospital setting. For example, most college admissions offices suggest business casual attire, but depending on the job interview, you may want to step it up from there. Again, it's important to do your homework and be prepared. In addition to reading up on the organization's guidelines, it never hurts to take a look around the website if you can to see what other people are wearing to work or to interviews. Regardless of the setting, make sure your clothes are not wrinkled, untidy, or stained. Avoid flashy clothing of any kind.

Even something like "business casual" can be interpreted in many ways,
so do some research to find out what exactly is expected of you.

Follow-Up Communication

Be sure to follow up, whether via e-mail or regular mail, with a thank-you note
to the interviewer. This is appropriate whether you're interviewing for a job
or student teaching position, or interviewing with a college. A handwritten
thank-you note, posted in the mail, is best. In addition to showing consideration, it will trigger the interviewer's memory about you and it shows that you
have genuine interest in the position or school. Be sure to follow the business
letter format and highlight the key points of your interview. Be prompt with
your thank-you note! Put it in the mail the day after your interview or send it
by e-mail the same day.

What Employers Expect

Regardless of the job, profession, or field, there are universal characteristics
that all employers—and schools, for that matter—look for in candidates. At

this early stage in your professional life, you have an opportunity to recognize which of these foundational characteristics are your strengths (and therefore highlight them in an interview) and which are weaknesses (and therefore continue to work on them and build them up). Consider these characteristics:

- Positive attitude
- Dependability
- Desire to continue to learn
- Initiative
- Effective communication
- Cooperation
- Organization
- Passion for the profession

This is not an exhaustive list, and other desirable characteristics include things like sensitivity to others, honesty, good judgment, loyalty, responsibility, and punctuality. Specific to education, you can add having empathy, flexibility, love of learning, and enjoying working with kids to that list. Consider these important characteristics when you answer the common questions that employers ask. It pays to work these traits into the answers—of course, being honest and realistic about yourself.

Beware the social media trap! Prospective employers and colleges will check your social media profile, so make sure there is nothing too personal, explicit, or inappropriate out there. When you communicate to the world on social media, don't use profanity—and be sure to use proper grammar. Think about the version of yourself you are portraying online. Is it favorable, or at least neutral, to potential employers? Rest assured: they will look.

FOR THE LOVE OF THE KIDS

Karen Canning started her professional life with a bachelor's degree in biology, working in a hematology lab. She then pursued a master's in business administration (MBA) and spent twenty years in the business world, working in the medical

Karen Canning

software industry. When her older son entered middle school, she realized she loved being around those kids and was drawn to middle school teaching. Because she already had her bachelor's degree, she took the Massachusetts state tests to qualify to begin teaching. She knew she wanted to work in middle school and started subbing at the nearby school. She then got a teaching position, got her master's degree in education, and has now been teaching seventh grade for fourteen years.

Can you explain how you became interested in being a teacher at a later point in your life?

I did consider teaching a long time ago, but I didn't think I had the patience. But after seeing middle school kids, there was something about them. They were funny and nice. I really liked them. I fit right in with those kids—I feel comfortable with them.

What is a typical day in your job?

This year, the admin wanted to tighten up hallway time and down time. At 7:30, we have a team meeting for thirty minutes; we address parents, grades, kids, and so on. I'm on the seventh grade team and with some specials teachers. We cover issues, procedures, and whatever comes our way.

At 8:00, the kids come in and we go to blocks, which are about fifty minutes each. I teach two STEM classes—eighth grade and fifth grade—and then the standard science classes for seventh graders. The day rolls very quickly. Kids leave at 2:18, but I am there until 4:30 or 5:00. During this time, we have some meetings with staff or I am preparing for the next day.

We have thirty minutes to eat lunch when the kids are eating lunch—the aides are caring for them during that time. We also have forty-five minutes of prep time in our contract during the actual day—that includes dealing with issues, planning purposes, making copies, submitting forms, creating an IP [IEP], and working collaboratively.

I grade papers and tests after school or I do sometimes bring work home, but I try really hard not to leave with papers to grade. Google Classroom and Forms have really helped in this regard, because exams and assessments are computerized, which has helped immensely with time management.

Last year, I had fifty-five seventh grade kids and forty STEM class kids. The STEM class was an elective for kids—not much homework. The seventh graders have Chromebooks and use an online textbook. Online textbooks have changed the dynamic of the classroom somewhat—student are staring at these books and are not necessarily on task.

Kids can look up terms and information these days. Instead of memorizing, I teach kids to be resourceful and curious. It's more about critical thinking and not about memorizing.

What is the best part of your job?

I love the kids! Absolutely! I love middle schoolers—they are funny, curious, innocent, and emotional. I just love them. You must tap into their likes and dislikes before you can try to teach them. The kids—that's the best part. I try my best to make a connection with each kid.

What is the most challenging part of your job?

The parents can be challenging. I am dumbfounded by how many parents are not supportive of their kids' education—kids who aren't doing well and don't have the motivation. I reach out to parents to get them on board to help, but I often get excuses instead. They don't help motivate the kids and don't think education is important. We have a lot of absenteeism—again, it goes back to the parents. What these parents may not understand is that kids learn discipline and motivation in school to push themselves, which helps them in life immensely. You can only do so much and if the parent isn't on board, it's hard to help that kid move forward.

To combat these issues, we try to communicate and have planned meetings with parents. We work together as a team to encourage parents and kids. We invite them in for meetings. We stay in touch with the principal and they can reach out to parents as well.

A good teacher is . . .

Very flexible. You can't be black-and-white. You have to be very flexible and be ready for unplanned things that come up. You must be able to think on your feet and make decisions right away. Sometimes you need a poker face and must seem unemotional and even hide your emotions. You don't want to show negative thoughts to your kids. Good teachers respect the kids. Also, you must be confident, or kids can mow you over and manipulate you otherwise. You have to hold your ground but also try to understand the kids.

Did your education prepare you for the job?

Yes, the business degree and the master's in education. I have used my MBA in my classes as well. I taught a year in middle school as part of student teaching. Since I was an adult and needed to make a living for my family, I was able to do the internship and make money, and that counted as my student teaching. I was observed just as a student teacher. Transitioning as an adult to teaching was pretty easy. I got a master's in three or four years—one course at a time throughout the years.

Has the job been what you expected?

Yes. Initially, when I first started, there was so much paper. Grading all that was long and difficult. Assessments aren't as aggressive and they pull out info and show what kids know quite as well. Teachers sometimes say there is too much paperwork, but it's manageable in my opinion.

What would be your advice to a young person who is considering becoming a teacher?

They have to love children. Focus on the children. If you can't deal with kids and don't love kids and don't want to understand them, you won't succeed. You have to figure out what ages of kids, too—they really are different beasts and have different needs. If you aren't ready to deal with all the kids, don't do it.

Take opportunities to get into a classroom and hang out and be an aide and work on projects with kids, so you can see what it's really like. Go to your counselor and ask about getting into a classroom—to start, just by observing. You can hang out with the kids and see what the class is like; that will help. Take the initiative to find schools that have a good education program and ask for help from your administration to get into those classrooms.

Remember that the content will change throughout the years, but that's not a big issue. You'll have to adapt and plan and present information in different ways. That's the easy part. Dealing with kids who are hurt or have family issues—or you get a report about a parent who's sick—helping those kids and supporting them is the challenging (and most important) part.

It's fun! Being with kids is fun! You've got to have a sense of humor and laugh at yourself.

═══════════

Personal contacts can make the difference! Don't be afraid to contact teachers and other professionals you know. Personal connections can be a great way to find jobs, student teaching positions, and internship opportunities. Your high school teachers, your coaches and mentors, and your friends' parents are all examples of people who very well may know about jobs or opportunities that would suit you. Start asking several months before you hope to start a job or internship, because it will take some time to do research and arrange interviews. You can also use social media in your search. LinkedIn (www.linkedin.com), for example, includes lots of searchable information on local companies. Follow and interact with people on social media to get their attention. Just remember to act professionally and communicate with proper grammar, just as you would in person.

Summary

Well, you made it to the end of this book! Hopefully, you have learned enough about the teaching field to start along your journey, or to continue along your path. If you've reached the end and you feel like teaching is your passion, that's great news. If you've figured out that it isn't the right field for you, that's good information to learn, too. For many of us, figuring out what we *don't* want to do and what we *don't* like is an important step in finding the right career.

With a little hard work and lots of passion, you can be a phenomenal teacher!

There is a lot of good news about the education field, and it's a very smart career choice for anyone with a passion for young people. It's a great career for people who get energy from working with children. Job demand is strong. Whether you decide to be a high school math teacher or want to focus on teaching first graders to read, having a plan and an idea about your future can help guide your decisions. After reading this book, you should be well on your way to having a plan for your future. Good luck to you as you move ahead!

Glossary

accreditation: The act of officially recognizing an organizational body, person, or educational facility as having a particular status or being qualified to perform a particular activity. For example, schools and colleges are accredited. *See also* certification.

ACT: One of the standardized college entrance tests that anyone wanting to enter undergraduate studies in the United States should take. It measures knowledge and skills in mathematics, English, reading, and science reasoning, as they apply to college readiness. There are four multiple-choice sections and an optional writing test. The total score of the ACT is 36. *See also* SAT.

associate's degree: A degree awarded by a community or junior college that typically requires two years of study.

bachelor's degree: An undergraduate degree awarded by colleges and universities that is typically a four-year course of study when pursued full-time, but this can vary by the degree earned and by the university awarding the degree.

cadet teaching/training: A specific career and technical education class at the high school level in which students interested in the teaching profession (usually seniors) are able to participate in organized, exploratory teaching experiences in kindergarten through ninth grade.

certification: The action or process of confirming that an individual has acquired certain skills or knowledge, usually provided by some third-party review, assessment, or educational body. Individuals, not organizations, are certified. *See also* accreditation.

classroom management: The methods and processes that teachers use to ensure that their classrooms run smoothly and that keep disruptive behavior to a minimum.

Common Core State Standards (CCSS): Developed by state governors and state heads of education, these standards define what K–12 students throughout the United States should know in English language arts and mathematics at the end of each school grade. The goal is to develop a set of internationally accepted standards that are used by every state. As of 2018, forty-two states have adopted and implemented these standards. (Oklahoma, Texas, Virginia, Alaska, Nebraska, Indiana, and South Carolina have not adopted the standards at the state level.) Most states began adopting the standards in 2014–2015. The standards were written to be demanding and to prepare students to compete in a global economy.

curriculum: The subjects or topics covered by a teacher that make up a course of study in a particular grade level.

doctoral degree: The highest level of degree awarded by colleges and universities. This degree qualifies the holder to teach at the university level and requires (usually published) research in the field. Earning a doctoral degree typically requires an additional three to five years of study after earning a bachelor's degree. Anyone with a doctorate degree—not just medical doctors—can be addressed as "Doctor."

elementary education degree: Typically a four-year bachelor's degree program that includes applicable coursework and student teaching experience that enables one to teach kindergarten through sixth grade.

English as a second language (ESL) teachers: Some teachers specialize in teaching ESL to elementary, middle, and high school students. They work only with students who are currently learning ESL and help them with assignments and curriculum from their standard classload. These students are often referred to as English language learners (ELLs). Also called English for speakers of other languages (ESOL).

gap year: A gap year is a year between high school and college (or sometimes between college and postgraduate studies) during which the student is not in school but is instead involved in other pursuits, typically volunteer programs such as the Peace Corps, travel, or work and teaching.

grants: Money to pay for postsecondary education that is typically awarded to students who have financial need, but can also be used in the areas of athletics, academics, demographics, veteran support, and special talents. Grants do not have to be paid back.

individualized education program (IEP): A written plan of action that addresses the specific educational needs of a child who is eligible for special education due to learning or attention issues. An IEP is developed by a team of educators to map out the services and curriculum needs of the particular child.

license: An official document, card, certificate, or the like, that gives you permission to have, use, or do something, such as practice as a teacher. Typically, one gets certified and then applies for a license.

master's degree: A postgraduate degree awarded by colleges and universities that requires at least one additional year of study after obtaining a bachelor's degree. The degree holder shows mastery of a specific field. Teachers in public school settings are often required to pursue their master's degrees after having worked as a teacher for a prescribed amount of time.

pedagogy: The method and practice of teaching.

personal statement: A written description of your accomplishments, outlook, interests, goals, and personality that is an important part of your college application. The personal statement should set you apart from other applicants. The required length depends on the institution, but they generally range from one to two pages, or 500–1,000 words.

postsecondary degree: An educational degree above and beyond a high school education. This is a general description that includes trade certificates and certifications; associate's, bachelor's, and master's degrees; and beyond.

private school: A school that does not receive support from government funding, such as local, state, or federal taxes. Because they don't receive public funds, private schools are not beholden to certain federal and state requirements and stipulations, such as teacher licensing and credentials. Students pay out of pocket to attend these schools. *See also* public school.

public school: A school that is funded by government monies, such as local, state, or federal taxes and grants. Students do not pay tuition to attend public schools, since they are funded by taxes. Public schools must meet state and federal requirements and stipulations, such as teacher licensing and credentials. *See also* private school.

SAT: One of the standardized tests in the United States that anyone applying to undergraduate studies should take. It measures verbal and mathematical reasoning abilities as they relate to predicting successful performance in college. It is intended to complement a student's GPA and school record in assessing readiness for college. The total score of the SAT is 1600. *See also* ACT.

scholarships: Merit-based aid used to pay for postsecondary education that does not have to be paid back. Scholarships are typically awarded based on academic excellence or some other special talent, such as music or art.

teaching assistant: An individual who works under the guidance of the main teacher to provide students with additional instruction. Teacher's assistants typically need to have completed about two years of college-level coursework to work in a classroom. Also called teacher's aide, instructional aide, paraprofessional, education assistant, or paraeducator.

Notes

Introduction: Careers in Education

1. Bureau of Labor Statistics, US Department of Labor, "Education, Training, and Library Occupations," www.bls.gov/ooh/education-training-and-library/home.htm.

Chapter 1

1. Bureau of Labor Statistics, US Department of Labor, "What Kindergarten and Elementary School Teachers Do," www.bls.gov/ooh/education-training-and-library/kindergarten-and-elementary-school-teachers.htm#tab-2.

2. National Center for Education Statistics, "Status and Trends in the Education of Racial and Ethnic Groups," https://nces.ed.gov/programs/raceindicators/indicator_rbb.asp.

3. Derrick Meador, "What Is the Difference between Teaching in Public vs. Private Schools?" ThoughtCo.com, last updated March 18, 2017, www.thoughtco.com/teaching-in-public-vs-private-schools-3194634.

4. Bureau of Labor Statistics, US Department of Labor, "What Middle School Teachers Do," www.bls.gov/ooh/education-training-and-library/middle-school-teachers.htm#tab-2.

5. Common Core State Standards Initiative, "Preparing America's Students for Success," www.corestandards.org.

6. Bureau of Labor Statistics, US Department of Labor, "What High School Teachers Do," www.bls.gov/ooh/education-training-and-library/high-school-teachers.htm#tab-2.

7. Bureau of Labor Statistics, US Department of Labor, "Middle School Teachers: Summary," www.bls.gov/ooh/education-training-and-library/middle-school-teachers.htm#tab-1.

8. Bureau of Labor Statistics, US Department of Labor, "Kindergarten and Elementary School Teachers: Summary," www.bls.gov/ooh/education-training-and -library/kindergarten-and-elementary-school-teachers.htm.

Chapter 2

1. Study.com, "How to Become an Elementary School Teacher," https://study .com/how_to_become_an_elementary_school_teacher.html.

2. Study.com, "Middle School Teacher: Requirements to Teach Middle School," https://study.com/teach_middle_school.html.

3. Ibid.

4. Indiana Department of Education, "Approved Transition to Teaching Programs," last updated November 13, 2018, www.doe.in.gov/licensing/approved -transition-teaching-programs.

5. Bureau of Labor Statistics, US Department of Education, "What Teacher Assistants Do," www.bls.gov/ooh/education-training-and-library/teacher-assistants .htm#tab-2.

6. Lou Adler, "New Survey Reveals 85% of All Jobs Are Filled Via Networking," LinkedIn, www.linkedin.com/pulse/new-survey-reveals-85-all-jobs-filled-via-network ing-lou-adler.

7. Mathew Hilton, "Leverage Your Volunteering Experience When Applying to Physical Therapy School," NewGradPhysicalTherapy.com, May 11, 2016, https://new gradphysicaltherapy.com/volunteer-experience-physical-therapy-school.

Chapter 3

1. Gap Year Association, "Research Statement," https://gapyearassociation.org /research.php.

2. Peter Van Buskirk, "Finding a Good College Fit," *U.S. News & World Report*, June 13, 2011, www.usnews.com/education/blogs/the-college-admissions-insider/2011 /06/13/finding-a-good-college-fit.

3. National Center for Education Statistics, "Fast Facts: Graduation Rates," https://nces.ed.gov/fastfacts/display.asp?id=40.

4. US Department of Education, "Focusing Higher Education on Student Success," July 27, 2015, www.ed.gov/news/press-releases/fact-sheet-focusing-higher -education-student-success.

5. Bureau of Labor Statistics, US Department of Labor, "How to Become a Middle School Teacher," www.bls.gov/ooh/education-training-and-library/middle -school-teachers.htm#tab-4.

6. Ibid.

7. Bureau of Labor Statistics, US Department of Labor, "Middle School Teachers: Summary," www.bls.gov/ooh/education-training-and-library/middle-school-teachers .htm#tab-1.

8. College Board, "Understanding College Costs," https://bigfuture.collegeboard .org/pay-for-college/college-costs/understanding-college-costs.

9. Federal Student Aid, US Department of Education, "FAFSA Changes for 2017–2018," https://studentaid.ed.gov/sa/sites/default/files/fafsa-changes-17-18.pdf.

Chapter 4

1. Justin Ross Muchnick, *Teens' Guide to College & Career Planning*, 12th ed. (Lawrenceville, NJ: Peterson's, 2015), 179–80.

2. Mind Tools, "Active Listening: Hear What People Are Really Saying," www .mindtools.com/CommSkll/ActiveListening.htm.

Resources

*A*re you looking for more information about the educational profession or even about a particular level of teaching within the profession? Do you want to know more about the college application process or need some help finding the right educational fit for you? Do you want a quick way to search for a good college or school? Try these resources as a starting point on your journey toward finding a fulfilling career in education!

Books

Banner, James M. *The Elements of Teaching*, 2nd ed. New Haven, CT: Yale University Press, 2017.

Bolles, Richard N. *What Color Is Your Parachute? 2019: A Practical Manual for Job Hunters and Career Changers*, rev. ed.. New York: Ten Speed Press, 2018.

Emdin, Christopher. *For White Folks Who Teach in the Hood . . . and the Rest of Y'all Too.* Boston: Beacon Press, 2017.

Fiske, Edward. *Fiske Guide to Colleges.* Naperville, IL: Sourcebooks, 2018.

Hougan, Eric. *Road to Teaching: A Guide to Teacher Training, Student Teaching, and Finding a Job.* North Charleston, SC: BookSurge, 2011.

Muchnick, Justin Ross. *Teens' Guide to College & Career Planning*, 12th ed. Lawrenceville, NJ: Peterson's, 2015.

Princeton Review. *The Best 382 Colleges, 2018 Edition: Everything You Need to Make the Right College Choice.* New York: Princeton Review, 2018.

Websites

American Gap Year Association
www.gapyearassociation.org
The American Gap Year Association's mission is "making transformative gap years an accessible option for all high school graduates." A gap year is a year taken between high school and college to travel, teach, work, volunteer, generally mature, and otherwise experience the world. The website has lots of advice and resources for anyone considering taking a gap year.

The Balance
www.thebalance.com
This site is all about managing money and finances, but also has a large section called Your Career, which provides advice for writing résumés and cover letters, interviewing, and more. Search the site for teens and you can find teen-specific advice and tips.

Cadet Teaching
www.teachercadets.com
A national career and technical education program, offered at the high school level, in which students interested in the teaching profession (usually seniors) are able to participate in organized, exploratory teaching experiences in kindergarten through grade 9.

Certification Map: Teacher Certification Made Simple!
www.certificationmap.com/states
This comprehensive site lists and explains the teacher licensing requirements in each state.

The College Entrance Examination Board
www.collegeboard.org
The College Entrance Examination Board tracks and summarizes financial data from colleges and universities all over the United States. This great, well-organized site can be your one-stop shop for all things college research. It contains lots of advice and information about taking and doing well on the SAT and ACT, many articles on college planning, a robust college search feature, a scholarship search feature, and a major and career search area. You can

type your career of interest (for example, elementary education) into the search box and get back a full page that describes the career; gives advice on how to prepare, where to get experience, and how to pay for it; what characteristics you should have to excel in this career; lists of helpful classes to take while in high school; and lots of links for more information.

College Grad Career Profiles
www.collegegrad.com/careers
Although this site is primarily geared toward college graduates, the career profiles area, indicated above, has a list of links to nearly every career you could ever think of. A single click takes you to a very detailed, helpful section that describes the job in detail, explains the educational requirements, includes links to good colleges that offer this career and to actual open jobs and internships, describes the licensing requirements (if any), lists salaries, and much more.

Common Core State Standards Initiative
www.corestandards.org
The Common Core State Standards (CCSS) were developed by various state governors and state heads of education as a set of internationally accepted curriculum standards that would be used by every state. As of 2018, forty-two states have adopted and implemented these standards as their proscribed teaching coursework.

Education Planner
http://www.educationplanner.org
This site—which includes sections for students, parents, and counselors—helps you break down the task of planning your career goals into simple, easy-to-understand steps. You can find personality assessments, get tips for preparing for school, read Q&As from counselors, download and use a planner worksheet, read about how to finance your education, and more.

GoCollege
www.gocollege.com
Calling itself the number one college-bound website on the internet, GoCollege provides lots of good tips and information about getting money and scholarships for college and getting the most out of your college education. The site also includes a good section on how scholarships in general work.

Go Overseas

www.gooverseas.com

Go Overseas claims to be your guide to more than fourteen thousand study and teach abroad programs that will change how you see the world. The site also includes information about high school abroad programs and gap year opportunities, and includes community reviews and information about finding programs specific to your interests and grade-level teaching aspirations, for example, information about the best countries for teaching English abroad.

Khan Academy

www.khanacademy.org

The Khan Academy website is an impressive collection of articles, courses, and videos about many educational topics in math, science, and the humanities. You can search any topic or subject (by subject matter and grade), and read lessons, take courses, and watch videos to learn all about it. The site includes test prep information for the SAT, ACT, AP, GMAT, and other standardized tests. There is also a College Admissions tab with lots of good articles and information, provided in the approachable Khan style.

Live Career

www.livecareer.com

This site has an impressive number of resources directed toward teens for writing résumés and cover letters, as well as interviewing.

Mapping Your Future

www.mappingyourfuture.org

This site helps young people figure out what they want to do and maps out how to reach career goals. Includes helpful tips on résumé writing, job hunting, job interviewing, and more.

Monster.com

www.monster.com

Monster.com perhaps the most well-known and certainly one of the largest employment websites in the United States. You fill in a couple of search boxes and away you go. You can sort by job title, of course, as well as by company name, location, salary range, experience range, and much more. The site also includes information about career fairs, advice on résumés and interviewing, and more.

Occupational Outlook Handbook

www.bls.gov

The US Bureau of Labor Statistics produces this website, which offers lots of relevant and updated information about various careers, including average salaries, how to work in the industry, job market outlook, typical work environments, and what workers do on the job. See www.bls.gov/emp for a full list of employment projections.

Peterson's College Prep

www.petersons.com

In addition to lots of information about preparing for the ACT and SAT and easily searchable information about scholarships nationwide, the Peterson's site includes a comprehensive search feature for universities and schools based on location, major, name, and more.

Princeton Review Career Quiz

www.princetonreview.com/quiz/career-quiz

The Princeton Review website includes a very good aptitude test geared toward high schoolers to help them determine their interests and find professions that complement those interests.

PRAXIS State Requirements

www.ets.org/praxis/states

PRAXIS tests are used by many state agencies to determine an individual's qualification to receive a license to teach in that state. Not all states use PRAXIS testing to grant licenses. This site includes a clickable list of US states and territories where you can find specific information about certifications and licensing requirements.

Study.com

www.study.com

Similar to Khan Academy, Study.com allows you to search any topic or subject and read lessons, take courses, and watch videos to learn all about it. The site includes many subjects that you could end up teaching, and is a great resource for your students.

Teach.org

www.teach.org

This site includes lots of information about becoming a teacher, including certification and licensing requirements, career paths, salary and benefits, funding your education, and more.

Teacher.org

www.teacher.org

This is a general site for all things related to earning a degree and becoming a teacher, including searchable job postings and other resources for aspiring teachers.

TeenLife

www.teenlife.com

This site calls itself "the leading source for college preparation" and it includes lots of information about summer programs, gap year programs, community service, and more. Promoting the belief that spending time out "in the world" outside of the classroom can help students develop important life skills, this site contains lots of links to volunteer and summer programs.

U.S. News & World Report *College Rankings*

www.usnews.com/best-colleges

U.S. News & World Report provides almost fifty different types of numerical rankings and lists of colleges throughout the United States to help students with their college search. You can search colleges by best reviewed, best value for the money, best liberal arts schools, best schools for B students, and more.

Bibliography

Adler, Lou. "New Survey Reveals 85% of All Jobs Are Filled Via Networking." LinkedIn.com. Retrieved July 8, 2018, from www.linkedin.com/pulse/new-survey-reveals-85-all-jobs-filled-via-networking-lou-adler.

TheBalance.com. "Career Choices," April 24, 2018. Retrieved August 10, 2018, from www.thebalance.com/career-choice-or-change-4161891.

Bureau of Labor Statistics, US Department of Labor. Education, Training, and Library Occupations. www.bls.gov/ooh/education-training-and-library/home.htm.

College Board. "Understanding College Costs." Retrieved September 2, 2018, from https://bigfuture.collegeboard.org/pay-for-college/college-costs/understanding-college-costs.

Common Core State Standards Initiative. "Preparing America's Students for Success." Retrieved August 24, 2018, from www.corestandards.org.

Federal Student Aid, US Department of Education. "FAFSA Changes for 2017–2018." Retrieved August 15, 2018, from https://studentaid.ed.gov/sa/sites/default/files/fafsa-changes-17-18.pdf.

Fiske, Edward. *Fiske Guide to Colleges.* Naperville, IL: Sourcebooks, 2018.

Gap Year Association. "Research Statement." Retrieved August 12, 2018, from https://gapyearassociation.org/research.php.

Go College. "Types of Scholarships." Retrieved August 12, 2018, from www.gocollege.com/financial-aid/scholarships/types.

Hilton, Mathew. "Leverage Your Volunteering Experience When Applying to Physical Therapy School." NewGradPhysicalTherapy.com, May 11, 2016. Retrieved December 20, 2017, from https://newgradphysicaltherapy.com/volunteer-experience-physical-therapy-school.

Hougan, Eric. *Road to Teaching: A Guide to Teacher Training, Student Teaching, and Finding a Job.* North Charleston, SC: BookSurge, 2011.

Keates, Cathy. "What Is Job Shadowing?" TalentEgg.ca. Retrieved August 21, 2018, from https://talentegg.ca/incubator/2011/02/03/what-is-job-shadowing.

Meador, Derrick. "What Is the Difference between Teaching in Public vs. Private Schools?" ThoughtCo.com, last updated March 18, 2017. Retrieved August 25, 2018, from www.thoughtco.com/teaching-in-public -vs-private-schools-3194634.

Mind Tools. "Active Listening: Hear What People Are Really Saying." Retrieved May 10, 2018, from www.mindtools.com/CommSkll/ActiveListening.htm.

Muchnick, Justin Ross. *Teens' Guide to College & Career Planning*, 12th ed. Lawrenceville, NJ: Peterson's, 2015.

National Center for Education Statistics. "Fast Facts: Graduation Rates." Retrieved July 10, 2018, from https://nces.ed.gov/fastfacts/display .asp?id=40.

———. "Private School Enrollment," last updated January 2018. Retrieved August 10, 2018, from https://nces.ed.gov/programs/coe/indicator_cgc .asp.

Study.com. "How to Become an Elementary School Teacher." Retrieved August 10, 2018, from https://study.com/how_to_become_an_elementary_school _teacher.html.

———. "Middle School Teacher: Requirements to Teach Middle School." Retrieved August 10, 2018, from https://study.com/teach_middle_school .html.

US Department of Education. "Focusing Higher Education on Student Success," July 27, 2015. Retrieved June 18, 2018, from www.ed.gov/news /press-releases/fact-sheet-focusing-higher-education-student-success.

Van Buskirk, Peter. "Finding a Good College Fit." *U.S. News & World Report*, June 13, 2011. Retrieved June 18, 2018, from www.usnews .com/education/blogs/the-college-admissions-insider/2011/06/13/finding -a-good-college-fit.

About the Author

Kezia Endsley is an editor and author from Indianapolis, Indiana. In addition to editing technical publications and writing books for teens, she enjoys running and triathlons, traveling, reading, and spending time with her family and seven pets.

CPSIA information can be obtained
at www.ICGtesting.com
Printed in the USA
LVHW012134051119
636387LV00008B/419